Jewish tradition is the oxygen that feeds these narratives and characters, so effortlessly and vividly. But what really delights here is the craftsmanship: Fine is a masterful author. The writing is naturally and warmly paced with gentle layers of insight and meaning in every story.

—Torey Malatia
General Manager, The Public's Radio

Michael Fine's The Jewish Prince of Denmark *is replete with engaging mystery, surprising curiosities, and delightful nuance. Open the door, step inside, and get ready to explore.*

—Frederic G. Reamer, Ph.D.
School of Social Work, Rhode Island College

A fine new collection of stories, and a fine welcome to Dr. Michael Fine's new tales. Wrapping his arms around a feast—mostly kosher—these helluva good stories are riveting, especially The White Donkey.

—Samuel Shem
Professor of Medical Humanities, New York University
Grossman School of Medicine. Author of *The House of God*,
The Spirit of the Place and *Our Hospital*

Michael Fine's fertile mind has generated inventively constructed intriguing tales in The Jewish Prince of Denmark. *Fine's creative word pictures offer vividly precise descriptions of reality and keen observations on history, politics, government, international affairs, family dynamics and the human condition. The stories aptly put forth epistemological, ethical and existential conundrums while grabbing the reader's attention with delightfully surprising twists and turns. Noting many of the absurdities and paradoxes in modern life, the book resonates with a sense of humor and healing, hopeful spirit."*

—Deborah H. Siegel, Ph.D.
LICSW, Professor Emerita, School of Social Work, Rhode Island College

PRAISE FOR
RHODE ISLAND STORIES

The best of the melting pot. Inspirational, big stories of many in the smallest state.

Michael Fine tells real stories of real people that make our community special. Telling Life experiences and life lessons that make an impact.

—Neil Steinberg
Former President & CEO, Rhode Island Foundation

These stories are a grand landscape of the outer State and also the inner "state" of its residents—the secrets, dreams, wisdom, foolery, struggles and triumphs. The Good Doctor Fine is brilliant in his writing, large in his canvas, and deep in his understanding. If R.I. didn't have a Poet Laureate, now's the time to start. This is a triumph.

—Samuel Shem
Professor of Medical Humanities, New York University
Grossman School of Medicine. Author of *The House of God*,
The Spirit of the Place and *Our Hospital*

The best part of our city, and our state, is the incredible culture and diversity that's not only very present but openly celebrated. Stories of challenge and stories of overcoming. Stories of hard work, of hope, of family, and so much more. Through an unfiltered lens, Rhode Island Stories *uniquely captures the depth of the narratives that often go untold, but quietly make up the very backbone of our communities.*

—Maria Rivera
Mayor, City of Central Falls Rhode Island

Michael Fine knows Rhode Island's people and places. He also knows what makes a good story. In this fine collection, he captures the hopes, dreams, fortunes and foibles of people across our quirky little state. You'll find someone you know here—maybe even yourself.

—Bill Harley
Singer, songwriter, storyteller, poet

Rhode Island Stories *captures the essence of Rhode Island's diversity and what makes our local communities so special, the people.*

—Donald R Grebien
Mayor, Pawtucket Rhode Island

Powerfully poignant, humane and embracing! Fine's latest work accomplishes what writers hope to do, but rarely accomplish...He opens the doors to many worlds, without interfering with any!

—Marc Levitt.
Documentary Film Maker, Writer and Educator

Dr. Fine peers into the ordinary lives of everyday people in his short stories that ask the question what if or why not. In my personal life and the multiple roles I play I often get lost in my own story fixated about the here and now without contemplating the bigger picture. When you read Dr. Fine's short stories they may also nudge you to think about your own life and what you can do to make this world a better place. This is a great read for those who are interested in stories placed in Rhode Island. For me the images of Rhode Island come alive in his stories and I believe they'll resonate for you too.

—Mario Bueno
Executive Director Progresso Latino

Dr. Michael Fine weaves together characters in stories in a way that reminds us that we have more in common than we have differences. Through his stories we are able to see ourselves as one people, indivisible after all.

—Nelly Gorbea
Rhode Island Secretary of State 2015-2022

PRAISE FOR
THE BULL AND OTHER STORIES

Physician, public-health leader, fiction writer and journalist Michael Fine's latest, and superb, book, The Bull and Other Stories, *displays his already celebrated mix of empathy tempered by an almost clinical realism; close observation of his characters' emotional, psychological, physiological and socio-economic circumstances, and their often contradictory values, all informed by his intimate study of American society and his acceptance of the ambiguities of memory.*

His portrayal of his characters' hopes, fears and confusions displays his deep understanding of how so many of us—especially those marginalized by poverty, illness and bigotry—live today. But Dr. Fine also impressed me with his acute observation of nature, be it forests, fields, flowers, the weather or non-human animals.

And there's plenty of suspense! Will the beast charge, will the tree fall on the forester, will the crazy woman stab her captives, will somebody shoot, will the demonstration turn dangerous? (There are some potential movies in this book....)

Dr. Fine is a major writer.

—Robert Whitcomb,
President, The Boston Guardian, Columnist for GoLocal24.com,
Former financial editor of the International Herald Tribune.

Michael Fine's world is not fair but it is full. His characters are not beautiful but they have dignity. In this rich collection of stories we meet immigrants and youth, elderly and laborers - all grappling with life as it is; full of societal conflicts, pressing pain, small graces, fleeting wonder and occasional hope. To read about them is to read about us.

—Chris Koller President
The Milbank Memorial Fund

The short story may be the most difficult of all fictional genres. In The Bull and Other Stories, Michael Fine, already a writer of great distinction, demonstrates he is a master. From first sentence to last, this collection is a rare delight.

—G. Wayne Miller
Author, Journalist and Filmmaker

The Bull and other stories, Rhythmic with a jazz cadence, poignant, timely and timeless, vivid detail but above all Michael Fine is a storyteller and a damn good one at that.

—Bert Crenca
Artist, Founder of AS220

Michael Fine's short stories rivet our readers in his monthly Sunday morning columns. We can imagine them sitting there with their morning coffee pondering the obvious and the not so obvious life dramas that Michael writes that capture you from the beginning, to the very end.

—Nancy Thomas
President of Tapestry Communications;
Co-Founder and Editor RINewsToday.com

This collection of stories takes hold and won't let go. The characters—including the bull and the oak tree—speak to the reader; you feel them. Lives are unvarnished—sad, banal, hopeful, sometimes all at once. Overwhelmingly real. Superb!

—Peter Nerohna
Rhode Island Attorney General,

THE
JEWISH PRINCE
OF DENMARK

AND OTHER STORIES

MICHAEL FINE

וַיָּבֹא־שָׁם אֶל־הַמְּעָרָה וַיָּלֶן שָׁם וְהִנֵּה דְבַר־יְהוָה אֵלָיו וַיֹּאמֶר לוֹ מַה־לְּךָ פֹה אֵלִיָּהוּ:

וַיֹּאמֶר קַנֹּא קִנֵּאתִי לַיהוָה ׀ אֱלֹהֵי צְבָאוֹת כִּי־עָזְבוּ בְרִיתְךָ בְּנֵי יִשְׂרָאֵל אֶת־מִזְבְּחֹתֶיךָ הָרָסוּ וְאֶת־נְבִיאֶיךָ הָרְגוּ בֶחָרֶב וָאִוָּתֵר אֲנִי לְבַדִּי וַיְבַקְשׁוּ אֶת־נַפְשִׁי לְקַחְתָּהּ:

וַיֹּאמֶר צֵא וְעָמַדְתָּ בָהָר לִפְנֵי יְהוָה וְהִנֵּה יְהוָה עֹבֵר וְרוּחַ גְּדוֹלָה וְחָזָק מְפָרֵק הָרִים וּמְשַׁבֵּר סְלָעִים לִפְנֵי יְהוָה לֹא בָרוּחַ יְהוָה וְאַחַר הָרוּחַ רַעַשׁ לֹא בָרַעַשׁ יְהוָה:

וְאַחַר הָרַעַשׁ אֵשׁ לֹא בָאֵשׁ יְהוָה וְאַחַר הָאֵשׁ קוֹל דְּמָמָה דַקָּה:

There he went into a cave, and there he spent the night. Then the word of GOD came to him: "Why are you here, Elijah?"

He replied, "I am moved by zeal for the ETERNAL, the God of Hosts, for the Israelites have forsaken Your covenant, torn down Your altars, and put Your prophets to the sword. I alone am left, and they are out to take my life."

"Come out," He called, "and stand on the mountain before GOD." And lo, GOD passed by. There was a great and mighty wind, splitting mountains and shattering rocks by the power of GOD; but GOD was not in the wind. After the wind—an earthquake; but GOD was not in the earthquake.

After the earthquake—fire; but GOD was not in the fire. And after the fire—a soft murmuring sound.

—I Kings 19:9-12

TABLE OF CONTENTS

THE JEWISH PRINCE OF DENMARK

She's lying somewhere in a pool of blood. I can see it. Clearly. A young Black woman as beautiful as a mink, her hair black, half braids, half that wet look that the young girls are wearing. It's Miss X (a well-known singer). She talks to me when she comes into the store. She comes into the store just to see me. We have a bond. She'd really like me to, well, you know, to take her out.

But I haven't given in to her yet. I'm waiting. We talk all the time. She tells me about her career, about her famous father and her almost famous sisters, about the record companies and the concert promoters.

I'm really kind of an advisor. She comes into the store for no reason at all, and buys little things—a bar of soap, a package of cigarettes—just so we can talk. You wouldn't believe what she says about her lovers. I think she's really coming on to me. It's a crazy world.

But now she's lying someplace in a pool of blood. I don't know how I know this. I just know. It's the little things. I hear hints under the breath of the announcers on TV. I've been seeing men with red hats everywhere I go, not something most people would notice or understand. Two days ago she was talking about going barefoot on a beach in Greece. Remember what happened with Sergeant Pepper, all the evidence that Paul was dead? Same story here.

And she hasn't been her usual self, like there's something freaking her out, like she's worried about something or someone that's too intense for her to talk about, even to me. She's only come in every other day or so for the last week. That's different for her.

She used to come in twice a day, maybe more. She hasn't been in at all for two days. Maybe she's mad at me, maybe someone told her something derogatory about me, some lie behind my back, like that I'm not really a genius after all. I'm certain she said she was going to be in town, that she was worn out from touring, from running back and forth from coast to coast. I don't understand it. No, I'm certain I'm right. There's just no other explanation.

So now I can't sleep. I can see her, just lying there. She's lying in a building that doesn't have any windows on the first floor. The floors themselves are wooden. It might be a loft. It might be a barn, but I don't see any hay. I'm walking up and down, back and forth in my room at night. I can't get it out of my head.

"Are you taking your medicine?" I ask.

I'm taking my medicine, your medicine, everybody's medicine. I'm taking the medicine you give me, sure, but look, it isn't that good, it isn't strong enough.

We have everything in the store. My father gives me things when I think I need something stronger. Valium. Haldol. Cogentin.

I don't like Thorazine, it makes me too sleepy, like a zombie, you know. I want to sleep, but I don't want to be, well, drugged.

"It's not a good idea to take medicine on your own."

Wait a second, I'm the one up all night, pacing the floors. What about Miss X? What are we doing for her? How can we help her? I called the police but they're corrupt, too busy to bother with the problems of Black people. What's a dead Black woman to them? One more number, that's all. They hate all the Blacks, they think all Blacks are garbage, they wish all Black people were dead.

I was thinking of calling the UN, or maybe the Russians or the Chinese, but I don't know, I'm not sure they'd understand.

"Why the Russians or the Chinese?"

They have something to prove. We're always going on about how much better we are then they are, how we have civil liberties and big cars and so forth, but it's not really true. It's all the same. A big lie. They have better social welfare, free medical care, no unemployment. We'll never do that. We like to let people suffer.

We have racism. A famous Black person, a famous African American woman singer is laying in a pool of her own blood and no one will do anything about it. If they looked into it and exposed us, it would look really bad at the U.N., and then maybe people would understand we're not what we're cracked up to be.

"But they have their own problems with human rights. Their own ethnic minorities. Isn't there a better country to talk to? The Scandinavian countries?" (He had mentioned the Danish delusion before, and I wanted to explore his thoughts about this in greater detail.)

Now there's an idea. You mean Denmark.

"Yes. Denmark."

I could call my father, I suppose. He's a very smart man, very busy. You know I was abused as a child, that they were too busy, and used to tie me in the closet. I have scars on my wrists to prove it. (He holds out his wrists, on which there are familiar looking scars.)

It wasn't necessary, him being royalty. But you don't believe the royalty part, do you? It's because you're Jewish too.

"Is your mother Jewish?"

Now she is. She had to convert to marry my father. But she's just my stepmother, see. My real mother was killed by the Nazis. She fought in the resistance. She was Jewish, on her father's side. Italian Jews, also royalty.

"When were you born?"

1948. You mean, how was my real mother killed by the Nazis, if I wasn't born until 1948? She was in Poland, after I was born, doing DP work. There were a few pogroms, nobody talks about them because it was after the war and Europe was a mess. The Poles took after the Jews who survived. They thought the Jews were getting better treatment. They blamed my mother. She was one of the last Jews to die in the Holocaust. Even though the Holocaust was over by then. It was very strange.

"I see." I wait. "Do you think this belief you have that you yourself are Jewish and that your real mother died in that way could have anything to do with the fact that I am a Jew and the child of Polish immigrants, concentration camp survivors?"

No, why? Oh, you mean the transference. No, sorry, that's really what happened to my mother. I'm not making it up, if that's what you mean. Why would I make it up? That's how my real mother died.

She was, I guess you'd call her a hero. I don't know why she's not famous, like Wallenberg. I think it's because of my father. They had to keep it quiet. Europe was a very complicated place after the war, and my father is a complicated man, lots of strange connections, strange friends, all suspect, all dirty, though I myself believe it was all for a good cause.

"I see."

You still don't believe me. (He signs, and waits a moment before continuing, uncertain that he can trust me. This distance is an obstacle to his progress that I have been unable to resolve.)

My father's family lived in Spain until the Inquisition. That's where the name comes from, why no one thinks I'm Jewish. They were merchants but very well educated people, advisors to the king of Grenada, I think, for what good it did them. When the Inquisition came, they fled to Portugal, then to Rhodes, in Greece, From Rhodes they found their way to Amsterdam. They established themselves in Amsterdam, in banking. Eventually, they set up a merchant bank that was to provide the capital for the first voyages to the New World. Then there was an argument—not over money, but over theology, something to do with Spinoza, who was a distant cousin. One branch thought he should be excommunicated, the other didn't, something like that. There were words, and one branch got sent to Denmark, to run the family business, a kind of exile. To everyone's surprise, the Danish branch did very well. Denmark was a backward county then, a place where no one could read or write, and the Danes had no understanding about banking at all. My father's great-grandfather became an advisor to the Danish king. Actually what happened was, he saved the country from bankruptcy, the whole country. My great-great grandfather and the king became close friends. They used to go out hunting. The Danish king made my grandfather a prince. It's an honorary type title. We can never become king or anything like that. But the title gets passed down from father to son, from generation to generation. I get it when my father dies. It's no big deal.

I haven't thought of calling the Danish embassy about Miss X. It's not a bad idea, but I don't think using influence would be fair. I want the police, the authorities to become involved because there is a life at stake, a human life. It's a terrible injustice.

The Chinese. I think I'll try the Chinese. The Russians, they have too much confusion right now, they don't know which end is up. The Chinese are trying to get back at us for getting mad about Tiananmen Square. This should be right up their alley.

"Our time is exhausted."

I know. You probably just think I'm crazy.

"What I think is of little importance. If you are unable to sleep, I suggest we meet again tomorrow at this time."

Sure, as long as it's after work. I hope Miss X comes into the store tonight. I'd sleep a lot better.

"I'm certain she will return. She is probably just out of town."

That night, I see a notice in a back page of the Times about Miss X, who I'd never heard of. She has disappeared, failed to appear for a regular booking, the police are involved, something about crank calls. Apparently Miss X is quite well known after all.

I begin to wonder, to worry. There is nothing in his history, nothing in his ego structure that would suggest danger or instability. I'm quite certain he would have discussed any homicidal ideation with me. He has always been open with me, amazingly open.

Then I replay our conversation in my head and recheck my notes. The image of a woman lying in a pool of her own blood, which comes up again and again. The repressed anger at the father, the abuse, the denied homoerotic identification with the therapist. Although my clinical judgment is that he is harmless, an objective analysis of this interview is disconcerting.

I decide to sleep on it, to discuss it with my supervisor in the morning. This was a privileged exchange. I can only violate his confidence if there is strong evidence of imminent danger to a third party.

On the other hand, what if this woman were to be hurt and my records were subpoenaed? I could be held accountable myself.

I myself am now unable to sleep. This case should not be affecting me in this manner. Countertransference? What conflicts in my own life, my own sense of self, are unaddressed? Is this guilt about superego lacunae?

I rethink my relationship to my own parents, who are well and live a few miles away, who I see weekly. Our relationship is fully formed, our major conflicts resolved. We have moved beyond adolescent conflicts long ago.

Some sort of misplaced guilt about the Holocaust? A Child of Concentration Camp Survivors' Syndrome? I have lived with the Holocaust all my life. I neither deny the Holocaust nor blame myself for it. It occurred before I was born.

None of this helps. Finally I rise from bed and decide to read.

Something takes me to a book about Sephardic Judaism, which traces refugees from the inquisition from Spain, through Portugal, to Rhodes and Amsterdam, and mentions a community in Denmark.

In the morning, before my first patient, I get a call from the Danish Ambassador, asking me questions I am not at liberty to answer.

The patient disappears. He misses his appointment. He doesn't answer his phone.

I call the store. He didn't come to work. Yes, Miss X was a frequent customer. The police have been by. Who am I? A friend.

Now I am completely unable to sleep. Now I lie awake nights, picturing the body of the beautiful Miss X, the blood dried beneath her. It is as if the blood is on my own hands.

I thought I *knew* patient X.

What have I done? What has been done in my name?

At last, I decide to warn Miss X. I call the police and refer to my credentials, my training. They send a detective to talk to me. He smokes without asking permission, acts like he's known me all his life, calls me 'Doc'. He listens. nods his head, shrugs his shoulders, but tells me I'm not really giving him anything to go on here. It'll be in the file, see, but there's no reason to think there's a problem, no evidence of foul play. This woman, she had a history, see. They are all like that. She probably ran off with her pimp. They're not like us, he says.

And then he winks, just in case my incredulous stare is serious, to let me know maybe he's joking, maybe he's just trying to throw me off the track. We'll look into it, he says. But they've had fifty calls a day on this one, from every nut in the city. Not that he means to suggest that I'm a nut, of course. He's got it all down, got the guy's address. They'll call me if they need to know more.

Weeks pass.
I don't sleep, certain I know the truth.
I am losing weight. My colleagues look at me strangely.

I go to his address. The woman who answers the buzzer never heard of him. No, she won't let me come up just to talk.

Some months later, I get a postcard from Greece, a picture of him standing on a beach with a beautiful Black woman on his shoulders.
They are both waving.

He looks a hundred times better than he looked when he was here.

THE GULF OF AQABA

They were risk-takers and everyone loved them for it. Richie took a sleepy little family hardware store in Weirton, West Virginia, and turned it into a multimillion-dollar enterprise with a mail-order business and stores in two hundred cities. Dvorah was from New York, from the Upper West Side. She was used to having everything at her fingertips, and everyone thought her thing with Richie, who was from the middle of no-place, was just a college fling until Dvorah went with him after college, first to West Virginia and then to Pittsburgh, which might as well have been Texas or Oklahoma or New Guinea, from the perspective of Dvorah's family and friends. And then she married the guy.

But even West Virginia and Pittsburgh couldn't slow Dvorah down. She was in New York every month; she kept dressing in a way that was to die for, and she'd light up a room like no one else when she came in on Richie's arm. The Met, Lincoln Center, Carnegie Hall, the downtown galleries as they developed, you name it, Richie and Dvorah were there. They went to Tel Aviv for a month each winter. It was hard to remember that they lived in Pittsburgh. They lived where they wanted to live and did what they wanted to do.

Their two kids were just like the parents. Day-school in Pittsburgh to be sure—that was Dvorah's doing—but then Sewickly, and Avi off to Dartmouth, with Dafna hoping for NYU or Yale. They both played soccer and played well—and they also knew their heritage. Both could read and speak Hebrew. Both knew trope and both could read Torah on Shabbos with just a little preparation. Dafna had a beautiful voice. She sang the female solo part during Shacharit on Yom Kippur, the part that sounds like it carries the congregation up to heaven itself while the doors of heaven are still open. Avi was just as accomplished on the soccer field. He played with confidence and with abandon and was the leading private high school scorer in Pennsylvania two years running. He competed for the US in the Maccabiah Games after his senior year in high school. Both children were like their mother, in that all eyes turned toward them whenever they entered a room. Any room.

Richie learned to fly, of course. He bought himself a little airplane and flew the family back and forth to New York, which was only a little more than an hour from Pittsburgh by air, and he flew to Florida once a month in the winter to see his parents who had a condo near the water in Sarasota.

So it was normal that, in November of 1991, they decided to go to Eilat instead of Tel Aviv or Vail for winter break. Eilat is a warm and beautiful place on the Gulf of Aqaba, close to Jordan, Saudi Arabia, and Egypt. You couldn't go to Petra yet. But you could go to Cairo if you were bold enough. Taba, just across the border but a little more than a mile away from Eilat, had gone back to Egypt in 1989 but the border was open and if you drove a few miles down the coast you could look across the Gulf at Saudi Arabia, which you could also see, clear as day, from the mountains just north of Eilat. Saudi Arabia! The place no Jew was permitted to be, home of Mecca and Medina, the location of the Haj. A mysterious, forbidden land. Just being that close whetted Richie's taste for danger, for adventure.

Peace, like the border, was so close yet so far away.

The strange baroque character of the human condition excited Richie. Historical enemies. A culture that hates us without even knowing we exist as individual human beings, with families and inner lives. The other. People with unfathomable minds, who walk in the hot desert in flowing white robes, their heads haloed in red-checked keffiyehs. Nomads on fast wiry horses. Kings and princes who have no interest whatsoever in democracy. Oil rich monarchs, who rule with the flick of a finger, who can condemn a man to death by simply raising an eyebrow. Unfathomable. Yet seductive. And just two miles away.

There is fantastic scuba diving off Coral Beach in Eilat. Amazing desert hikes. Day trips to Saint Catherine's Monastery on Mount Sinai itself, the place the Greek Orthodox call God-trodden and Arabic speakers call Jubal Musa. Great beaches. Great hot sun, even in January.

In 1991, Israel still held the West Bank, Gaza, and the Golan Heights, captured during the Six Day War in 1967 and held during the Yom Kippur War of 1973. Israel had returned the Sinai Peninsula to Egypt in 1982 after the Egypt-Israeli Peace Treaty of 1979 but held on to Taba, a little strip of land along the Gulf of Aqaba, until 1989, when it reverted to Egypt, except for a few hundred yards of what is now called the Coral Beach Nature Reserve. In 1992, Yitzhak Shamir was the Prime Minister of Israel. George H.W. Bush was the president of the US. The Gulf War, in which the US and its allies took Kuwait back from Iraq, had ended the year before. The First Intifada, which had begun in 1987 on the West Bank, was winding down. It exposed the difficult lives Palestinians led under the Occupation, but it likely made their day-to-day life worse. The Madrid Peace Conference had just ended. The UN adopted resolution 46/86, which revoked UN Resolution

3379. Zionism was no longer a form of racism, according to the UN, which meant Jews and Israelis felt a little less bitter about their place in the world, for the moment—although nothing had improved for Palestinians living in the West Bank and Gaza.

To the extent there was peace between Israel and its neighbors at all, it was a cold peace, a suspicious peace, the peace of no overt warfare, a peace that included occasional terrorism across borders, expressing animosity, anger, and fear. The Arab world and the Arab Street supported the Palestinian people in their struggle. The Jewish world supported Israel and entrained the US into supporting Israel as well. No one could figure out how to end the Occupation in a way that let Israelis feel safe and secure, understanding that to Israelis, whenever a Palestinian lifted a gun, it was Adolf Hitler and three millennia of other enemies pulling the trigger, and to Palestinians, whenever they were stopped at a checkpoint, it was because outsiders—the Crusaders, the Turks, the British, their landlords in Beirut and Cairo, and now Israel and America—had taken their land and freedom, and boxed them in for generations, this people who only wanted to go about their lives and be left alone to make their own decisions and choose their own destiny. Without invaders in their midst.

Of course, none of that mattered in Eilat. Eilat was a sleepy little resort town of twenty-five thousand souls by 1992, a place that had many more visitors than residents. Israelis from the north, who came in the winter looking for sun, and Swedes, Danes, French, Norwegians and others, who came for the cheap accommodations by the beach, along with Russian Jews, half-Jews, one great-grandfather-Jew and non-Jews, who came by the thousands once the Soviet Union started to fall apart in late 1989, to stay at hotels along the beach and sleep on the beach. Eilat became a place for sun and holiday, like Miami Beach, Blackpool, Sevastopol, Yalta, or Cannes.

People came to lie in the sun, not to think, argue or fight. The chaos of the real world stayed far away. That the little airport, with its terminal right in the city itself, just off the beach, had runways that ran parallel to the runways of the Jordanian airport of Aqaba a few hundred yards to its east but just over the border, seemed of no consequence. That the Jordanian city of Aqaba, which was three times the size of Eilat, lay a few hundred yards to the east on the other side of a border that felt impenetrable, seemed of no consequence either. Eilat was a playground and meant to stay that way. A good place for the Goodwins to spend three weeks and wait out the return of sunlight in Pittsburgh and of Fashion Week in New York. That Saudi Arabia, a major belligerent and a desert fortress shrouded in mystery, was just a few kilometers south, seemed of no consequence at all.

So it was a shock to everyone who knew them when they heard the news. When they read about it in all the newspapers. When it was all over the TV. The Goodwins had been out on a boat in the Gulf of Aqaba, eating, fishing and scuba diving, when a motorized rubber dingy appeared, moving fast across the water. Three terrorists, armed to the teeth, a Jordanian/Palestinian and two Saudis. They overpowered Richie and Avi. And slit the throats of all four of the Goodwins, dumping their bodies in the water. Then they took the Goodwin's boat to Coral Beach and shot a security guard dead before they themselves were overwhelmed by the IDF and were all shot dead on the spot. One more senseless tragedy in a chain of senseless tragedies, linking two peoples together in an endless litany of sadness, anger and hate.

In an instant the Goodwin family was wiped out, their lives and their legacy gone from the face of the earth forever.

The first question, after Jonathan Levin's heart was ripped out of his body, twisted like a dishtowel being wrung out, and stomped upon; after he managed somehow to pick up his heart and put it back into his chest, was how to think about the last terrifying moments of his sister and her family, now lost forever, the victims of a conflict they had nothing whatsoever to do with themselves. The second question was what to do next, who had to do it, and who was in charge.

There is no guidebook that tells you what to do when your sister, her husband and her two beautiful children are murdered, no set of directions, no rules to follow. A building collapses on you. There are no written directions on the box telling you what to do next. The State Department called. Jonathan had no idea how they found him. Then five minutes later the Israeli Ministry of Defense called. And then five minutes after that it was the three major networks plus CNN. About five minutes later Jonathan's friend Rob called to say that the street in front of his house was filled with the TV trucks. Then there were TV lights bathing Jonathan's house, and someone ringing his doorbell every thirty seconds. How are the kids going to get to school in the morning? Jonathan remembered himself thinking. Even though their school was just around the corner on Sessions Street. And what will the neighbors think? Even though Jonathan already knew what the neighbors were thinking, which is what he would have been thinking had the situation been reversed—they were thinking about this awful tragedy, were thankful it wasn't them or their kids, and were damning a violent world and its senseless cruelty and violence.

"No comment," was all Jonathan could say at first. Somehow, Rob Marsh, who Jonathan davened with, his lawyer and a trusted friend, appeared and handled the press. Somehow, he told Joanna. Somehow, they gathered their three young children together, and told their children about a tragedy that was too much for any child to know about, let alone to bear. Somehow Jonathan broke free and called his mother, who was living in the Hebrew Home for the Aged in Riverdale, and heard her say the Shema, and be thankful that his father was no longer alive to hear this news. Somehow. Somehow. Somehow.

Even so, and regardless of what they were thinking, their friends and neighbors appeared. They mobilized and clustered around Jonathan and his family, a herd of elephants circling a wounded calf. The community went into high gear. They took care of Joanna and Jonathan's three young children. They fed them and held them and stayed with them. They were there and would stay until the enormity of what had just transpired faded just a little into everyone's memory, a memory which would be forever cloaked in a sadness of infinite depth.

She is a beautiful woman, his big sister, Jonathan thought. Was a beautiful woman, Jonathan had to tell himself. Was. Past tense. No longer is. No longer living.

But Jonathan still couldn't believe it. Didn't believe it. Wouldn't believe it. There must be some mistake. How could this be? Are you sure? Could they have the name wrong? Couldn't this little family vacationing in Eilat have been mistaken for another little family? Sure there must be hundreds of little families of the same name, the same ages, some also Americans, out diving in Eilat that day. But not. Of course not. It was before cell phones, so Jonathan couldn't pick up his phone to dial Dvorah's number, just in case.

It was later, although how much later Jonathan couldn't say because time had vaporized, that Jonathan put in a call to Richie's sister, who lived now in Berkeley, California.

The sister was, how does one say this? a little different. They knew one another, of course, Jonathan and the sister, from family events. The rehearsal dinner and the wedding. The bris and the naming. The Bar Mitzvah and the Bas Mitzvah. The sister had come to all of them. Most of them. Some of them. Mostly alone. Her husband and kids never came. There was a husband and kids, three adopted kids, that's it, in Berkeley California. Jonathan couldn't quite remember if Richie's sister had come to Jonathan and Dvorah's father's funeral. He didn't think so.

They weren't close, Richie and his sister. Richie's sister, Joanie, that's it, didn't do Thanksgiving, Pesach or Rosh Hashanah with the family. It was too far to travel, that was the explanation, the excuse made in passing whenever someone asked after Joanie's health.

Joanie had orange hair flecked with gray that came halfway down her back, hair that she sometimes wore in braids, pale skin and freckles. She was tall and thin, almost too thin, and had a tentative expression, frightened or always unsure—it was hard to tell—and she never looked at you when she spoke to you. She was partial to long shapeless flowery dresses and self-righteous sounding statements about inequality, racism and social justice, always framed in a way that made it sound like she was the only person on earth who cared about those ideas, and she was the only person on earth who could tell the difference between right and wrong. She was married to a philosopher, a tall spacey looking man who didn't appear to have shoulders, who was balding but had long hair, who was overwhelmingly and intentionally gentle, who wore flannel shirts or t-shirts everywhere and seemed to float from place to place, who bounded, instead of walking, with a huge rocking stride. They had adopted three children, one each from Haiti, Eritrea, and Vietnam.

Jonathan was pretty sure that Richie's parents were still alive. He remembered that they lived half the year in West Virginia but spent winters in Sarasota at a senior living condo development for New Yorkers, walking the beach and talking about the day's New York Times. The father was mentally hazy now. The mother was okay. She was a decent human being, a woman who worked in her husband's store her whole life and made big family meals, big boisterous seders and big Thanksgiving dinners. Which her daughter, Richie's sister, stopped attending when she went off to Berkeley and left the earth for the stratosphere. Jonathan assumed they knew by the time he remembered to call Joanie. Everyone knew. Everyone in the universe knew. A billion or two people all around the globe heard the sound bite about the murder of Jonathan's sister and her family together, about this, their personal disaster, and all those people heard about it at the same time. For everyone else, it was someone else and too bad, such a tragedy, really. But for Jonathan and everyone he loved it felt like all the light had gone out of the world and was never coming back.

What Joanie remembered about Rich was his courage, which sometimes felt like recklessness but usually felt like arrogance. He was the younger brother. He was supposed to know his place, to be shy and respectful. But that wasn't Richie. He acted like there was no one else in the room except him, that what he thought and felt mattered, and that no one else, not their parents, not aunts and uncles and grandparents, not teachers or scoutmasters or coaches or even his bigshot friends mattered. Joanie had learned the rules about how to be a child of Jews in Weirton, West Virginia and she tried to teach those rules to Richie. But Richie ignored her. He ignored those rules and all rules. But none of that mattered now.

When they were really little, before either of them could read, Joanie pretended to read to her little brother, who was a pudgy little kid with black hair and olive skin, whose complexion made him look like they had different parents. Joanie memorized the words in picture books and would recite what she remembered as she turned the pages. She expected Richie to sit quietly in her lap and listen, the way Joanie listened when their mother or father read to her. But Richie never sat still. He'd take the book out of Joanie's hands and turn it upside down, and then turn the pages and tell his own story in baby talk, as if Joanie wasn't there, as if she didn't matter.

Joanie never thought Rich would amount to anything. He broke his leg when he was eleven when he flipped over a minibike he was riding in the woods, and from then on everyone doted on him. His friends all came and signed his cast. Then they took turns pushing him through school in the wheelchair until he figured out how to work the wheels and then he started racing his friends down the hall. He never handed in assignments on time. Joanie, who was her high school's valedictorian, got near perfect grades and had perfect handwriting. All the teachers looked at her as the perfect student, that funny looking Jewish girl who listened and never talked back. Richie was the wild brother, the kid who was always testing the limits. It was a miracle he got into college at all. He lasted one semester at Ohio State. He came back home to Weirton, and Joanie thought he'd end up a used car salesman, a bank teller, a drug addict or in jail. Then he started working in the store and the rest was history. First there were two stores. Then ten. Then mail-order. And then Richie was the star, and Joanie, well, she went to Berkeley in the mid-seventies and almost never came home again.

Even so, Richie was the only brother Joanie had. The brother who stayed in West Virginia and took care of their parents, so Joanie didn't have to. The brother who made sure that his parents had a place to go on Thanksgiving and on the Jewish holidays, even if he had to fly their parents to New York, which meant Joanie never had to give her parents a second thought.

I'll go to Sarasota to be with my parents, Joanie thought. It's the least I can do.

Eilat. In Israel. My brother the Jew, who thought the rules

didn't apply to him, Joanie thought. Who thought the world didn't notice what goes on in the West Bank and Gaza. We didn't grow up like that. We didn't fly airplanes or go scuba diving. We had a little hardware store in the middle of nowhere. We were just average people, like everyone else. Not royalty. Not venture capitalists. Not rock stars. Never people who profited from the misfortunes of others.

And then Dvorah's brother Jonathan called from Rhode Island. He was a doctor, a gastroenterologist, Joanie thought. Wife and three little kids. Observant Jew. Lived in Providence, Rhode Island, down the street from a synagogue and JCC. In tears. As different from me as night and day.

"Ha'makom yenahem etkhem betokh she'ar avelei Tziyonvi Yersuhalayim. May G-d...comfort you...along with all the mourners... of Zion and Jerusalem" Jonathan said, trying to speak and hold back his tears.

"To you as well. I'm sorry for your loss," Joanie said.

"Our loss," Jonathan said.

"Our loss. I can't believe it," Joanie said.

"It's... Do your parents know?" Jonathan said.

"They do. I'm on my way there. I have a flight from Oakland in about an hour. Your mother?" Joanie said.

"She knows. I'm only glad my father..." Jonathan said, but couldn't continue.

"The state department...." Joanie said.

"They called," Jonathan said. "And the Israeli Ministry of Defense."

"Me too. They called. I talked to them. Anyway. This should not have happened. They should never have gone..."

"It's up to us now. They need one spokesperson for the family," Jonathan said.

"You can speak for your family. I'll speak for mine," Joanie said.

"That's not what.... Whatever is best for you. My friend Rob, my lawyer has been handling the press here. He could..." Jonathan said.

"No lawyers. They only make trouble and they charge by the instant," Joanie said.

"We're going to need some legal help sorting everything out Joanie. We can do this together," Jonathan said.

"You do your family. I'll do mine," Joanie said. "I'll be making a brief statement of my own."

"Joanie some decisions have to be made... quickly. We can do this... together. You and I. Your parents. My mother. We are all... next of kin," Jonathan said.

"Which means we all have an equal voice. Or vote. Or whatever," Joanie said. "Equal. That means no one is better than anyone else. No domination by history or gender. None of that," Joanie said.

"They were an observant family, Joanie. You know that," Jonathan said.

"So that?"

"So that funerals need to be in twenty-four hours. Or as soon as possible. We need a place for the funerals, and graves, and I have no idea what they planned for themselves. I can't believe we are having this discussion. I can't believe it... I don't know if there are graves, do you?"

"I don't know. Maybe my parents know. We haven't discussed it. I can call you when I get to Sarasota," Joanie said. "My family isn't like that. Observant. Richie didn't grow up that way. And I don't do any of it. Religion makes more trouble than it's worth. Wars. Hatred. Refugee camps. The occupation," Joanie said.

"Do you know who Richie's lawyer is? For the business? I know they had a will," Jonathan said.

"I have nothing to do with the business," Joanie said. "Richie took a little hardware store, a community business that served poor and working people for a hundred years and made it into a huge corporation. I'm sure he had lawyers. Lots of lawyers. And bankers. That's the trouble, isn't it? People think they can rule the world, that they can jet here and there, that they are invincible. They think other people's lives don't matter. But you know what? We all die of something. We're all equal, in at least that way."

"We have a family plot. In Queens. Our side is all in New York. Or used to be. Their friends were in Pittsburgh. Is there anyone left in Weirton? People you grew up with? Your parent's old friends?" Jonathan said.

"I was born there. But that's all. Everyone died or moved to Florida. All the kids moved to DC, Boston or New York," Joanie said.

"Where are your grandparents buried?" Jonathan said.

"In Weirton," Joanie said. "In the Jewish section of the cemetery. No that's not right. The Jewish cemetery is in Steubenville. Steubenville, Ohio. Just across the Ohio River."

"How far is Pittsburgh?" Jonathan said.

"About half-hour," Joanie said. "A little more. Depends on traffic."

"What do you think about a funeral and shiva in Pittsburgh?" Jonathan said. "Their friends are there. The kids' friends. We need to take care of them too."

"I'm not ready to make any decisions now," Joanie said. I want to talk to my parents first. I don't know what my parents can handle. I don't know if they can make the trip. It's January."

"We need to move quickly Joanie," Jonathan said. "We need to sort out the funerals and the burials and the Shiva. I'm the, I was the kids' guardian... in case their parents...." Jonathan said, and then he broke down.

"What?" Joanie said. "I don't know anything..."

"It's in their will, I think," Jonathan said as he sobbed. "Richie, Dvorah and Joanna and I talked about the guardianship piece. I thought you..."

"I don't know anything about any of that. Typical. Typical of my brother. The golden boy. Never a thought about anyone but himself. Joanie is in Berkeley and she doesn't matter. Never mattered. Only boys matter."

"*None* of that matters now Joanie. We have a job to do. An obligation. A duty. We're who's left. We have to take care of..."

"It's all too little too late, isn't it? Generations of violence, of exploitation, of oppression. Think that's going to go away by saying we are sorry?"

"Can we..."

"Arrange your funerals. Pick your gravesites. Set up your shiva. I have a plane to catch. I'll call you in the morning from Florida," Joanie said. She slammed down the phone.

What was that? Jonathan wondered.

Jonathan sat alone in his attic study looking down on the street. A man walked a dog. He and the dog entered a circle of light cast by the streetlight nearest Jonathan's house. Then the man and the dog walked through the light and faded into the darkness. A few snowflakes dusted the night air, falling at an angle because of the cold wind.

Jonathan had never felt himself so alone. So bereft. So desolate. The world had changed from a stable and secure place to a place that was hostile and tragic. It had become a place without hope.

After it was all said and done, after they buried Richie and his family, after the shiva and the will and the lawyers and the accountants, after the inheritance tax was paid and the issues around the corporate board and the foundation board were settled, Joanie assumed she would never see Jonathan again, which was fine with her. They were different people. They lived in different worlds. The will was clear. It didn't matter much, anyway, not really. Everyone was okay financially before. So there was really nothing to fight over. The tragedy was the tragedy. A catastrophe, Joanie thought, recognizing the irony: the Palestinians call Israeli independence and their exodus and diaspora the Nakba, the Catastrophe. The murder of Richie and his family in a terrorist incursion was just that catastrophe, brought home and made real to Americans and to American Jews. Even if they weren't listening. So sad that it involved Joanie's own family. But the world isn't always fair and it is certainly far from just. That that goes around comes around. Still Joanie would have preferred that cruel fate had picked on someone else, that particular day.

Once or twice a year, Joanie found herself in Washington, DC, usually to lobby for one organization or another. She'd combine those trips with visits to her parents and would fly to Florida from DC if the trip was in winter. If the trip was in the spring or summer, she'd rent a car and drive to see her parents in Weirton, which is about two hours from DC.

You couldn't really call what Joanie did lobbying. The organizations that mattered—Women United to Prevent Gun Violence, Mothers for Public Education, and USCPR—The US Center for Political Redemption—called these visits Hill Week, and every organization in the nation does these visits, which exist mostly to justify the organizations' existence. You fly in and they put you up in a Dupont Circle hotel or at the DC Hilton, which was where Reagan got shot. They have a briefing session, in which they give you talking points about a particular bill or budget item that the organization wanted Congress to pass or approve. They'd have a friendly senator or representative drop by the hotel for a cocktail hour and a brief talk about the politics of the day, about who was up and who was down and why nothing was moving through Congress right at the moment, which was always because of the intransigence of the other party.

Then they'd drive you to the Hill in buses and you'd fan out to visit the offices of your particular senator or representative. Most of the time your particular senator or representative had just been called to the floor for a vote or was in committee, so you'd meet with a twenty-seven year-old squeaky clean looking legislative aid, who was almost never from California but had gone to Georgetown or BU or Villanova, a college with a good basketball team, and the young legislative assistant would half listen to your pitch and then give you their boss's position on your talking points, which made it sound like their boss agreed with you and hoped your legislation would move but always stopped short of committing to it or signing on as a sponsor, which was what you to came ask for. "I'll tell you what we can do," the young LA would always say, and then would give you some information that you didn't need or send you to a website that wasn't helpful and that you knew about already. Joanie had been down this road a hundred times. She knew and the organizations knew and the LAs knew and the actual lobbyists knew that these visits don't ever change one thing.

Even so Hill visits are an important part of the culture of Washington. They keep the organizations, the lobbyists and the LAs employed, and they help provide everyone with the illusion that something important was happening in Washington, even though nothing really changed. Of course no one ever really thought about the suffering of the poor, the corruption and selfishness of the rich, the pain and suffering of the sick, or the loneliness of most Americans during those Hill visits. Joanie knew someplace inside her that government exists to keep things as they are, not to create meaning or justice. And that knowledge kept her sad but also humble when she came to DC. She knew not to get her hopes up, not anymore, despite all the marching, letter writing and demonstrating.

It was early March 2008, nineteen years after Richie, Dvorah, Avi and Dafna were killed. Washington's weather wasn't much different from the weather in Oakland at that time of year. Oakland had been cold and rainy all winter, but the cold in DC was a harsher cold, without the brilliant sun and warm breezes you sometimes get in the Bay area in the late afternoon. It was dark and raining. There was still ice and slush on the streets. Some of the flowers were up, dark green stems pushing aside dull brown earth, but nothing had bloomed yet, not even the crocuses.

It bothered Joanie that her hotel was filled with Orthodox Jews. At least she *thought* they were Orthodox. The men wore yarmulkas, but they weren't crazy people, not the kind who wear black coats and big hats and the men didn't have those fringy things hanging from their belts like the Jews Joanie sometimes saw in Oakland, the kind who drove around in minibuses with loudspeakers and who stopped men on the street, hoping to get them to pray. The women were tastefully dressed, often in business suits or in skirts and sweaters. These Jews looked like businesspeople, low-level executives, or doctors and lawyers, and they hurried from place to place, attending meetings of their own. They gathered in conference rooms at the hotel in the morning and evening for little prayer sessions during which they put on black and white prayer shawls and swayed back and forth with their heads buried in prayerbooks, or sang together in Hebrew, sometimes reciting prayers Joanie distantly remembered from childhood. Who were they? Why were they in DC?

AIPAC, that's who they were. Joanie saw a sign on one of their buses and it explained everything. The American Israel Public Affairs Committee, the enemy, the other side. AIPAC was an organization of American Jews that used the lobbying power and political might of the American Jewish community to lobby for Israel, to secure American support and money for whatever Israeli government was in power, regardless of their policies or positions. Israel in a war?

AIPAC gets the US to send planes and bombs and block any criticism of Israel at the UN. Israel wants to annex Palestinian land? AIPAC lobbies for the US to look the other way, and block, or try to block, UN sanctions. Israel bombs Gaza again and kills a thousand people, including lots of kids which it calls "collateral damage"? AIPAC makes sure all Americans know about every single rocket fired on Israel from Gaza, which then mostly missed their targets and fell harmlessly on farmers' fields. Except the ones that didn't, the ones that killed people, mostly innocent elders and children. And so it was, continuously for the last 70 years. If Palestine isn't an independent state yet, Joanie thought, it's because of AIPAC and these clean looking people who all look like they have MBAs.

Jonathan was standing in the back of an elevator at the hotel as Joanie entered, and his gaze met hers as she looked up before turning around. He had seen her first and placed her. It took her a moment to figure out who he was.

"Hello Joanie," Jonathan said quietly. "How are your parents and kids?"

"Jonathan. Hello Jonathan," Joanie said. "What are you...well I guess I know. AIPAC, right?" Joanie said.

"Yup," Jonathan said. "Every year. But surely you..."

"No not me, Joanie said. "Happenstance. I'm here for Hill Week. Women United to Prevent Gun Violence. You know the drill. Then off to see my parents."

"They're well?"

The elevator door opened.

"My floor," Jonathan said. "Let's catch up." He thrust a card into Joanie's hand as he walked by. Then he was gone.

Painless, Joanie thought. One and done. Figures he's with AIPAC. Just figures. No one ever learns from experience, no matter how sad. No one ever listens. No one ever changes, and so we are left with this mess, the consequence of our selfishness, intransigence, narcissism, and greed. The good news is that I never have to see him again.

The rain started at midday the following day and by mid-afternoon had become a drenching cold rain that was unrelenting. Joanie finished up the last of her congressional visits at the Cannon Building at one, and found her way to the corner exit, a long block from the Metro. She looked around for a cab to take her down the block but there are never any cabs in that part of Capitol Hill, south of the mall. Good public transportation is a mainstay of democracy, she thought, and she was glad to have an umbrella, even though her raincoat, shoes and stockings were soaked by the time she had taken fifty steps.

A gust of wind flipped her umbrella inside out as she came out of the Metro at Farragut Square, so she was completely wet by the time she reached her hotel. Her hair was wet, her chest and back were wet, there was water dripping down her face and her glasses had fogged.

She'd checked out of her hotel in the morning and left her luggage with the bellhop. Change in the ladies' room, she thought. And then a cab to National Airport, which had another name that Joanie still would not use.

She borrowed a hairdryer from the desk and changed in the bathroom. And then went rushing out to find a cab. Her flight was at four-thirty. Just enough time. Barely.

It was still pouring. Connecticut Avenue was bumper to bumper, the brake lights and the headlights of the red Washington cabs reflected in the windshields of cars and trucks, in the windows of stores and restaurants and even by the water on the street, reflected by the pavement which had become slick and glossy like the cover of a magazine. Horns honked and doors slammed. There was a line of people waiting for cabs, perhaps ten people in front of Joanie, all wearing hats scarves and overcoats, their collars raised against the wind and rain. They all held umbrellas even though they were standing under an awning. Joanie looked at the people in front of her and tried to guess how many were together, how many parties of two and three were waiting together. I'm never going to make my plane like this, she thought, and considered the Metro for a moment but couldn't bear the thought of getting drenched again walking to the Metro in the rain.

The man getting into the first cab turned to open the car door. Jonathan.

Joanie knocked on the window of the cab as Jonathan was giving his destination to the driver. The bellhop, Jonathan thought at first. I must have left something. Instead it was a woman, a beautiful woman, truth be told, her freckled white face and graying red hair wrapped in a green kerchief.

"I'm late getting to the airport. Are you going to National?" Joanie said.

Jonathan recognized Joanie's voice before he placed her face. The memory of that voice was wrapped in huge fathomless pain but the voice itself was an instant cue.

"Oh Joanie," Jonathan said. "Sure. Yeah. National. Reagan. No problem. Room for two." And paused. "Driver, can you pop the trunk? More luggage," Jonathan said, loud enough to be heard through the plexiglass partition.

"I really appreciate this," Joanie said after she had settled herself into the seat next to Jonathan and closed the door.

"No problem," Jonathan said. "Especially you. Family. More or less," Jonathan said.

"By marriage," Joanie said.

"Yeah, by marriage," Jonathan said. "More or less."

The cab's springs bounced a little as the cab came down the hotel driveway and into the street. They swayed together as the cab made a U-turn and headed south, holding up traffic as the driver nosed into a line of cars that wasn't moving. Horns blared but the driver didn't turn. Instead, he raised his right hand, gesturing, as if to say, *give me a break everyone. I have to make a living too.*

"Doesn't look like we are going anywhere fast," Jonathan said. "What time is your flight?

"Four-thirty. Yours?" Joanie said.

"Six-thirty. You meet half of Rhode Island on that flight. Senators. Congressmen. Business owners. Everybody. We all know each other."

"You know, I feel like I don't really know *you*," Joanie said.

"There's not much to know. And it doesn't matter much now," Jonathan said.

They fell silent. The cab inched forward, barely making one car length each time the traffic light in front of them changed. The cars from the cross street blocked the avenue. There was a policeman in a yellow rainslicker blowing a whistle and waving his arms in the intersection. But there was no room to maneuver.

"Things get better south of the White House," Jonathan said after a few minutes. "Once you get into one of the tunnels,"

"I know. I try to fly into and out of National whenever I come to DC," Joanie said. "The airport is like, three to four miles from the Capitol, maybe less. I love flying in over the White House and Capitol, over the Washington Monument and the Jefferson Memorial. Pretty stirring despite all the mess."

"What mess?" Jonathan said.

"You know, the mess that this country is always in," Joanie said. "Iraq and Afghanistan and the racism and immigrants and the Middle East. Endless messes. Politics. That mess."

"Oh," Jonathan said. "That mess. I don't see it as a mess, exactly. I see it as a country that is extraordinarily lucky, that is finding its way in the world, feeling its way in the dark, if you will, trying to figure out how to be better. That guy Obama just won the democratic primary in New Hampshire, didn't he?"

"He won the caucuses in Iowa. And came in second in New Hampshire," Joanie said.

"Gave a pretty good speech up there," Jonathan said.

"Come on," Joanie said. "This country will never elect a Black man president of the United States and you know it. Just window dressing."

"I don't know Joanie," Jonathan said. "Our grandparents came here as immigrants a hundred years ago. The country has been pretty good to us."

"I wish it were equally good to everyone," Joanie said." We can pass. People of color can't pass."

"You think? Hard to confuse me with a tall blond guy wearing lime green pants who went to Yale," Jonathan said.

"Didn't you go to Penn?" Joanie said.

"Point taken," Jonathan said.

They fell silent again. The driver turned left but nothing was moving.

"I'm afraid you are going to miss your plane," Jonathan said.

"Probably," Joanie said. "But the time difference works in my favor when I fly East to West. A long as I can get out by midnight, I can get home today."

A cellphone rang and the driver answered it. He spoke rapidly in another language. Arabic? Farsi? What language did they speak in Ethiopia? Amharic? How about in Eritrea?

Suddenly the cab stopped. The driver opened his window. The driver of another cab, moving in the opposite direction stopped and opened his window. The drivers talked even though there was space to drive forward in front of each cab. Talked loud in that other language. Or at least in another language that Jonathan couldn't understand.

Then the driver rolled up his window and swung the cab around, stopping next to the curb behind the other cab, which had pulled over. He turned around.

"You pay now," the driver said. "Get out now. Bad tire."

"Are you crazy?" Jonathan said. "It's pouring rain."

"You get out now. Pay now," the driver said.

"Why would I give you one penny?" Jonathan said. "You haven't gotten us to the airport,"

"Pay fare on meter," the driver said. "Pay now."

"I'm not understanding you," Joanie said. "Is there something wrong?"

"Bad tire. You get out now. Pay now," the driver said.

A man appeared next to Jonathan's window outside the cab. It was the driver of the cab parked in front of them. He was carrying a baseball bat.

"This isn't a cab ride," Jonathan said. "It's a hold up. Or a kidnapping."

With that, the doors on both sides of the cab locked. The driver of the other cab stood outside next to Joanie, his bat raised like a club.

"Let me pay you," Joanie said, and she opened her purse. "How much?"

"Put your purse away, Joanie. They want you to take your wallet out so they can grab it."

Joanie didn't put her purse away. But she didn't take her wallet out either. She rummaged around in her purse.

"How much?" she said.

"Two hundred dollar. Cash now," the driver said.

"I don't carry that much cash. Let me find my wallet. Jonathan, do you have one-twenty? I'm looking in my purse. I keep my cash in a hidden compartment. I think I might have eighty."

"Are you nuts?" Jonathan said. "They have your luggage in the trunk. Pay them now and they'll take your purse and everything in the trunk and we'll never see them again."

"Now. Pay now. Get out now," the driver said.

"I know. You don't negotiate with terrorists," Joanie said.

"Who the fuck do you think you are?" Jonathan said. "I'm calling the DC Taxi Commission." Jonathan leaned forward to see the driver's picture and license which was displayed on the dash.

Jonathan pulled his cell phone out of his top pocket. But the driver pictured on the dash was a man wearing a turban who didn't look like the driver at all.

Two quick loud thuds. The cab shook. Glass everywhere. The window next to Jonathan shattered, spraying glass fragments across the back of the cab.

Then suddenly, DOO-OP DOO-OP DOO-OP, right behind them. Brilliant white, red and blue lights everywhere.

The driver threw his door open and bolted.

Then there was a cop leaning over next to Jonathan, asking if they were okay.

Later, they sat together in a restaurant at the airport. They had both missed their flights and had three or four hours to kill.

"So you weren't going to give that guy cash?" Jonathan said.

"No. Not even close," Joanie said. "I was buying time. My cell was in my purse. I was feeling around for it. I dialed 911 while you were talking. I hoped and prayed that the 911 operator would hear you talking and send help."

"Good move. Got us out of a jam. Quick thinking. I didn't know you were much for praying, though," Jonathan said.

'Manner of speaking," Joanie said. "I use language figuratively. I'm not a fundamentalist."

"You think?" Jonathan said. "You know Joanie, I'm not a fundamentalist either. Science is okay with me. So is justice. We just have different ways of thinking about things, different ways of getting from point A to point B."

"I'm sorry about how I acted," Joanie said. "When Richie and Dvora and the kids got killed. So selfish. So doctrinaire. What I said at the funeral was what I believed. What I still believe. But that wasn't the time or place."

"You were in shock. We all were. I'm still in shock. After all these years," Jonathan said, and his eyes filled with tears.

Joanie put her hand on Jonathan's hand. And her eyes filled with tears as well.

"There is injustice in the world. Selfishness and greed," Joanie said.

"And anti-Semitism," Jonathan said.

"And anti-Semitism, but the world doesn't turn around the Jewish people, however much Jews have suffered. Other people suffer too. "

"And that suffering is our fault?" Jonathan said.

"The challenge is to keep bending the arc of the moral universe toward justice, despite the selfishness and stupidity of human beings," Joanie said.

"I thought you had given up on Judaism," Jonathan said. "You sound like Hillel, Rabbi Nachman or the Bal Shem Tov."

"All men, right?" Joanie said.

"All men, Joanie," Jonathan said. "Good men. The world survives because of good people—Jews, Christians, Muslims, Hindus, whatever. Men and women. Who make moral choices. Who on some days balance the evil that exists among people as well. Maybe. A little. For now."

"Hey, we were a good team in there, in that cab," Joanie said.

"A good team," Jonathan said. "I can't say I knew what position I was playing, or even that we were in the game, but history is told by the survivors, yes? By the victors and the survivors."

"Us, I'm afraid," Joanie said. "The next of kin."

They stood to go. That part of the airport is dark and cavernous. The passageway in front of them had been filled by people rushing by to catch planes, people wearing raincoats that were still wet from the driving rain. But now it was late, and the terminal was deserted.

They hugged. Then they headed for different gates, understanding that they would probably never see or hear from one another again.

THE NOBODY

She was a nobody, a flirt who was still unmarried at thirty-one when the Germans came back in 1939, and can you believe it, she was probably glad when they returned, at least at first. Hannah Singer had been only seven the first time the Germans came, in 1915, but she thought the Germans were so much more polite than the Russians and the Poles, and so much better looking. At seven, Hannah didn't understand wars or politics, of course, and didn't understand the meaning of the words and ideas that were thrown about then—The Kingdom of Poland, the Czar, the Central Powers, Zionism, the three partitions, Socialism, Communism, Bolsheviks, Archduke Ferdinand—because who among us, even then, knew what was good or bad for the Jews? The Poles didn't have real uniforms and their clothes were often muddy. The Russians were boors. They drank too much, swore and spat in the streets and acted like they had a right to take what they wanted, even though they didn't seem to know what street they were on or where they were going. But the Germans had nice manners. Please and thank you. They would hold the door for a woman, even a

Jew. They asked permission to come into a store or business to look around. And we could usually understand them, more or less, even though the language they spoke seemed so formal and stiff.

In any case, the Russians disappeared when Hannah was a girl, even though we still called where we lived Russia-Poland. Hannah, who had a gift for languages, remembered Russian anyway. She learned German, formal German, while the Germans occupied Mazovia. We could all speak a little Polish, maybe even more than a little, which we used when the working people and farmers came to Biezun on market days, but we didn't speak it at home unless someone was telling a joke. Treif. Unclean. Polish felt unclean. Yiddish was the mamaloshen, the mother tongue. We lived and breathed and prayed and thought and joked in Yiddish, even though we spoke other languages. Hannah spoke Yiddish, of course, and read Hebrew. She learned Spanish and French in the Gymnasium. Seven languages. Most of us only spoke three or four languages, and only one or two well. That's how it was. Our life then. Complicated. The life that had been given us. We didn't give any of it a second thought.

Hannah was ten when the Germans disappeared in 1918. Later, we learned that the Central Powers had intended to empty Mazovia of Jews and Poles and settle Germans from the Eastern Provinces in what were then our homes, after they won the war. What the Central Powers planned was nothing, of course, compared to what the next German government planned, and did. Who could have imagined?

Even in Mazovia, there were ethnic Germans who lived alongside the Poles and the Jews, for hundreds of years. The Jews were innkeepers and grain dealers. The Germans were bankers and bureaucrats. And Poles worked the land. Nobody remembered how Germans and Jews came to be in Mazovia, how we each were allies of the Polish kings, once upon a time, and had been sent to subjugate and modernize a backward land of peasants and drunken noblemen who had allied with the Polish Church, and how we each were the wedge those kings used to split the church and the nobles apart, and wrest power away from local people, to create riches for themselves. Except the Poles. The Poles remembered. Someplace deep inside themselves. They saw our granted rights, our separate laws and our courts and even the miserable lives we eked out with the very limited franchises we had been given as privileges that had been taken away from them by guile and the force of arms, and they never forgot. Then, we thought to ourselves, the Poles are a sad people to be avoided, even if they are our neighbors, our customers, sometimes our friends and sometimes even lovers. To Hannah, and to the rest of us, the Germans were the people of culture and of modernity, and we looked up to those Germans, both those who lived nearby as our neighbors and those who came in uniform in 1915 and then left again after the Armistice, as the people we wanted to be.

Hannah was the youngest child of eight, a golden girl. Her maternal grandparents (my grandfather's brother was her grandfather's cousin) owned inns in Ciechanow and Plonsk and stables in both places. People of means. They set her parents up in business in Biezun, as dry goods merchants and dealers in vodka in a little market town twenty-five kilometers away that was surrounded by wheat fields. The rich earth made for good harvests. The farmers came to Biezun on market days, and all Hannah's father had to do was to be in the right place, on the right day, keep stock on his shelves, and he could make a living.

Maybe it was Hannah's mother, who had grown up around a little money and had high expectations of a better life. Maybe it was living in a small place and meeting those German soldiers, who had such nice uniforms and good manners and spoke politely during the war years. Maybe it was the children she played with in that small town, the children of the banker and the clerk of courts, who were as different from the Poles as Hannah was but in a different way. Whatever it was, Hannah came out flighty and insubstantial. She chattered on and on. She liked pretty things. She spoke perfect German and a good Polish and even a decent Russian, but she never read a book.

Not that life was any picnic during the first war. Shortages. Men conscripted for labor. Horses requisitioned. Stores emptied in support of the war effort. People went hungry enough to eat uncooked groats. But the Germans were different from the Russians in Galicia. They knew not to starve and kill us and drive us to support their enemy. We survived. That Jews were starved and murdered or chased out of Galicia by the Russians wasn't lost on us. That Austria, the one country to our east and south that gave Jews the time of day was German speaking wasn't lost on us either.

Girls didn't go to study then the way boys did. Boys went to cheder from age three in Radzanow and from age ten to yeshiva in Raciaz. But girls learned at home or in the local public school and then only until age twelve. Reading and writing. Sewing and simple arithmetic. In bigger places the Jewish community had schools for girls and the children of working people, but Biezun had only a little synagogue and a little mikvah but no school. The girls learned siddur Hebrew from the rebbetzin in the synagogue after the public school was done.

But the local school wasn't good enough for Hannah. She was a nobody in her school. She wore pretty dresses. She flitted from place to place and made friends with the German kids and the Polish kids, as if there was no difference between us. She chattered on in those languages and she even began to look like the other children in Biezun. She didn't have blond hair, exactly. But she played outside in the spring and summer, and her brown hair lightened and developed chestnut streaks. She never had the brooding expression, or downcast eyes of the rest of her people. We were visitors in this land and we knew it. Mazovia had only opened to Jews a hundred and fifty years before, and some cities and counties were still off limits. The Church hated and feared us. We could all be gone in a minute, and somewhere in our souls we knew that. But Hannah didn't seem to understand, as if our lives and our history didn't apply to her. She was a lightweight, a butterfly, pretty but insubstantial. And that was all she wanted from life.

Then one day in 1918, without warning or explanation, Hannah was gone. She had gone to live in Ciechanow with her grandparents and go to Gymnasium. A Jew from Biezun, studying at a Polish gymnasium with the Polish and the German girls! Haskalah thinking had infected our communities thirty years before. Yeshiva students from all over Poland rebelled, threw over their traditions and went to work in factories and write socialist tracts. Or started smoking cigarettes and wearing berets. Or went off to America. Or became labor Zionists, learned to farm and went off to Palestine. So we were used to a certain amount of disruption. But a young girl from Biezun, going to a Polish gymnasium where she'd learn French and read Goethe? All of us expected to see her come back in a Daimler limousine, wearing furs, on the arm of a blond man. If she ever came back at all. Bad enough that she had no substance. Worse that she would soon be lost to her family, our people and our history.

So we forgot about her. The first war ended. The Germans went away. The Second Polish Republic came into existence in November 1918 and Pilsudski came back from exile. The Russians didn't come back to Poland until 1939, and they never came back to Mazovia. Some of our cousins left for America and Canada. Others went to Argentina. One or two went to Palestine after all. For five minutes we thought Poland might be good for the Jews again.

For five minutes. Then Lithuania attacked Poland, Russia attached Poland, the Ukraine used its own five minutes as an independent nation to attack Poland, and Czechoslovakia attacked Poland, and everyone who was anyone formed a political party, and all the parties began to fight with one another.

Hannah disappeared from our lives. As the years passed, we heard this and that, whispers about a romance with a financier and an army officer after the Coup. And then something about singing in the Opera. But no wedding. No husband and family. Nothing. No word. She was nobody we thought about anymore.

This happened in our families from time to time. And it was exactly what we expected, knowing Hannah as she grew up. It wasn't that there wasn't a brain in the head or a heart in the chest. It was more like there was nothing Hannah needed to do, and no reason for Hannah to make one choice or the other. As if she had no memory, no conscience, no history, no connection and no guilt. She spoke seven languages. She could be whomever she wanted to be, whenever she wanted to be that person. Or nobody at all.

And then, in 1938, just before the world came apart, a different Hannah returned to Biezun. She came alone. She lived in her parent's house, which was the largest house in our town, a yellow wood frame house with a big porch just off the town square. The rest of the Jewish community lived on and around Ciechanow Street as it went east—small squat wooden houses, packed together, nestled in little lanes and back alleys just before our little town emptied into the wheat and barley fields that surrounded us. The synagogue and mikvah were around the corner, on the far side of the town square, just steps away. The town hall was on the square as was the Catholic Church, which was made of stone and by far the biggest building in town. Our lives were paced by its bells, which rang on the hour and rang most on Sundays and on market days.

Hannah appeared in Biezun late one fall, just after the days had shortened. We saw her sitting on one of the rough-hewn wooden benches in the town square on days when there was no market. Or we saw her sitting on the porch of her parents' house. She wore the plain dark dresses and square black shoes of the observant women and of the Polish war widows who were called to Mass every morning by the bells. She had her own hair, not a wig, so it wasn't like she'd become observant and married. There were rumors of a love affair with one of Pilsudski's colonels, a married man, and of a child who had died in infancy, but that's all they were, rumors. Hannah didn't talk much and she certainly didn't talk about her life.

Sometimes a woman would join her on the bench in the town square, a German woman who had also gone to Gymnasium in Ciechanow.

Hannah was at the table when her large and boisterous family sat down for Shabbos dinner or on Rosh Hashanah or at Pesach, but she didn't talk much. Her younger cousins watched her with a certain kind of awe. She had gone into the world and returned. She was lost to us but came back, not like the cousins, aunts and uncles who had gone off to America, Canada, Argentina or Palestine, and who didn't come back but sent letters and packages and stories of their lives in those places. Not like them at all. What did all this mean?

By the time Hannah returned, however, we were filled with foreboding. Pilsudski died in 1935 and the National Democrats, the Endejka, with their quotas, their cold pogrom and their young thugs, returned. It was impossible to ignore what was going on in Germany, in that elegant, sophisticated, modern nation just to our west, which gave encouragement and succor to the many anti-Semites in Poland, and was a difficult distraction to a disorganized, hungry nation that yearned for a strongman, that wanted control and order more than it wanted diversity, modernity and light.

Pilsudski made a deal with the Nazis in 1934, the German Polish Non-Aggression Pact. Then Krystallnacht happened in November of 1938. We worried about Hitler and the Jews, of course. But Germany was still another country. We had plenty of anti-Semites at home. And it was still the Depression, so not everyone had enough to eat.

Sometimes Hannah could be seen in the back of the synagogue, in the women's gallery for Mincha-Maariv, the afternoon and evening prayers, not davening, not praying, but just sitting quietly by herself. She'd leave before the others, so almost no one knew she had been there. Almost. On those late fall and winter nights, she could be seen walking home under the huge elms that grew around the town square as the new electric lights came on, and as the bells from the Catholic Church tolled six times.

And then disaster. 1939. The German Polish Non-Aggression Act turned out to be Hitler's idea of a joke. Hitler and Stalin made a secret pact on August 23, 1939 and partitioned Poland again for the fourth time, dividing it amongst themselves.

One week later, on September 1, 1939, the German tanks rolled into Mazovia. By September 4th the Germans had gone past Biezun and taken Ciechanow on their way to Warsaw. On September 10th the Einsatzgruppe V was looting Jewish homes and synagogues in Ciechanow. They arrested several hundred Jews as well as the local intelligentsia, such as it was—schoolteachers, priests, ministers, and postal clerks and lawyers—took them to the village of Oscislawo, machine gunned them all, and then buried them in a mass grave. By October 6th Poland had been conquered and divided again. There was no surrender. Just annexation—the west went to Germany, the east to Russia, with little pieces chipped off for Lithuania and Slovakia.

We saw the bombers flying over. It took only two weeks for the Germans to appear in Biezun, after the Gestapo set up shop in Ciechanow and Plonsk. We went about our business. We were a little town, not very important, surrounded by wheat fields, on no major road. For a while we thought the Germans might just forget us. But that was not to be.

The Germans remembered the plan for Mazovia made during the first war, the plan to empty Mazovia of Poles and Jews so that it could be given to Germans from the west, and so Mazovia's wheat fields could feed the Reich and the Aryan race. So the Gestapo came to Mazovia first. In late October a German truck with loudspeakers rolled into Biezun, followed by two troop carriers. The voice over the loudspeaker ordered all Jews to the town square. The trucks parked in front of the synagogue. Not that there was anything unclear about who the Gestapo was and what they wanted.

Register first. Give us a list of every man, woman, and child. Armbands and a big yellow star to be worn on the left chest and back. The Jewish stores and businesses were all immediately closed.

We were going to be moved to Ciechanow. That's what we heard. We put on the yellow stars and we stayed in our homes. Young men roamed the streets at night drunk, calling to one another, sometimes saying our names, sometimes saying the names of the Jewish girls they knew.

In October they arrested the schoolteachers and all the seventeen- and eighteen-year-olds, Jews and Poles alike, and took them away. They cut the salaries of all Jews who earned a salary by sixty percent. We could only go to the market for an hour, on Tuesdays. That first winter there were still apples, potatoes and carrots from the gardens, of course, from our own gardens and the root cellars of the peasants and wheat farmers, but the apples, carrots and potatoes were all gone by spring.

When we had to go out, we walked quickly, with our heads down.

We knew about the concentration camps in Germany and how Jews were sent there after Krystallnacht—but that had happened in Germany, a different country, until it wasn't. Some people believed that Warsaw was safer. I don't know why. Some people fled east, hoping to cross the border with Russia. But there really was no escape. Our parents wrote letters to family in Argentina, Canada, England, and America. Coded messages. *Thank you for telling us about your recent success. We hope to see you in the New Year,* the letters said. *Send bread and salt,* the letters said. *Do anything and everything you can to get us out. Now. We are starving,* the letters meant. But Hitler got his hands on the post office and stopped the mail of the Jews. They called that *postsperrem.* Block the post. Those letters never arrived.

It didn't matter.

The winter of 1939 into 1940 was long and cold. The wind howled into Biezun from the wheat fields. There was still a little wood that could be bought and burned but no coal—the Nazis took it all.

But the spring wasn't real to us that year. Spring has little meaning when you are locked in your own house and can't see branches get red and then grow leaves in the thickets, or see the grass turn green, or let the sun fall on your arms or back or walk without shoes in the brooks and streams that are teeming with newts and salamanders, with pollywogs and then frogs and toads.

We didn't think about it when we saw Hannah walking by herself after sunset. She had a dark bonnet and a dark grey cape. She kept her head down, stayed close to the houses and walked in the shadows of the roofs as she walked from house to house. She walked in the town square as she always had, but she walked there under the huge elms just a few minutes before dusk, just before the lights came on. Later, when the Gestapo turned the lights off, she walked under those elms after dark as well. When you saw her, just a shadow moving quickly to avoid the light, when you saw a little movement out of the corner of your eye, you wondered if you had seen a ghost. When you looked, nobody was there.

Sometimes in the middle of the night, in the hours just before dawn, before even the birds awoke, after the moon had set or on nights with no moon, a truck would come down the Ciechanow road slowly, without headlights. In the morning a house would be empty. We didn't speak about it. The choices weren't good ones. Run to Warsaw. Safety, perhaps in numbers. Perhaps. But people were starving in the Warsaw Ghetto. Beg or buy a carrot or a potato or steal a chicken. Find a farmer to hide you. Hide in the woods. Or stay, be deported, and die.

Then one night just before Pesach in April of 1941, after we had survived more than a year and a half of living on air, on a knife edge, there was a soft knock on the door after midnight, the knock of a gloved hand. We lived in fear of the pounding on the door of the Gestapo, who would come to interrogate with the least provocation, after a Jew had been seen talking to a Pole or, perish the thought, to a German; after a gallon of gas had gone missing from a petrol station; when a Jewish mechanic was caught working on the car of a Polish policeman; when a Pole had been seen near the Jewish section with two pounds of flour, more than the allotment for his family—or after a family had disappeared.

"Wer ist da?" said my father, who was still awake, whispering in German. *Who's there?*

"Keyner," whispered the voice back, in Yiddish. *Nobody.*

My father opened the door.

"Hannahala!" he said, and rushed Hannah inside.

It was a different Hannah. This Hannah was thin, like the rest of us. She wore the grey cape and the dark hat we had seen her in at dusk when she walked close to the buildings. No yellow stars. She looked right at my father, which was something women didn't ever do then, look directly at men who weren't their husbands, but there was no time to waste. She needed him to hear her and move quickly.

"Tonight," Hannah said. "Now."

"To where?" my father said.

"The Red Forest is safest. But we can try for Warsaw. The Gestapo is in Ciechanow and Plonsk. The ghetto in Nowy Dwor is no better. You know that."

"And there are people?..." my father said.

"There is no one." Hannah said. "I can get you out of Biezun. After that you are on your own. But winter has passed. You work with your hands. You will go under a truckload of straw. The Nazis can't eat straw. Not even them."

"To the Red Forest, then," my father said. He turned to my mother. "Wake and dress the children," he said, not realizing I was already awake.

"I am a Russian woman," Hannah said. "With four Russian children, who is in Poland twenty years, married to a Jew I met during the last war, when he fought for Austria. My husband is in the Strzegowo Ghetto. You found me by accident, through a cousin who lives in Radzanow, when you were trying to sell furniture and learned I knew someone with a truck. You don't know my name or where I live."

"I understand," my father said.

"Who arranged all this?" Hannah said.

"Nobody," my father said. "Nobody I know."

Hannah came with us in the truck. She sat with the driver. She had removed her hat, and put on a bright red kerchief over her hair like the kerchiefs that wives of Polish farmers preferred.

We arranged ourselves under the straw. All we took with us was a satchel or two for clothing. We took a hatchet and knives and matches and candles and enough food for two days, and we each wore three changes of clothes, one on top of the other. The truck drove without headlights until dawn, when it turned into a side road and pulled off the road under a grove of trees. And we jumped out.

My father never got a chance to ask Hannah anything about what had happened in her life, or what brought her back to Biezun. What had changed her? We would never learn the answer to that question.

We found a thickly wooded little hilltop near a farmer's field about two days' walk from where we had been dropped, and built a shelter for ourselves out of rocks, branches and tree-bark, and dug into the hillside to make a cave for ourselves in a rocky north-facing ravine far from any road. We carried water from a stream at the bottom of the ravine. We learned to steal a little from the fields of surrounding farms—a little, enough to feed ourselves but too little for the farmer to notice. We learned to eat tree bark and grass and learned how to trap squirrels and eat snakes. My mother, who spoke a good Polish, would walk up to farms, claiming to be a Polish woman whose husband was a schoolteacher and had been shot by the Gestapo, looking for work. The suffering of the Polish people was like our suffering, only different. Sometimes she brought back a chicken. Most often they shooed her away, afraid of who she might be, or just afraid.

Hannah likely died in November of 1942. The remaining Jewish population of Biezun was moved to the Ghetto in Ciechanow in July of 1942. Most of the 4500 Jews of Ciechanow had already been shipped to labor camps or other Ghettos and would end up in Auschwitz. In November of 1942 all the remaining inhabitants of Ciechanow Ghetto, 1800 souls, were marched into the Red Forest, machine-gunned, and then buried in a mass grave. We heard the gunfire and then the earth movers, but we didn't go to look.

One day in March of 1943 my father went out to scavenge for food and never came back. Sixty years later, when the archives of the Ciechanow Gestapo were opened for public view, I learned that my father had been murdered by a Polish farmer, clubbed to death as he was trying to steal a spring lamb, and then buried in a shallow grave.

My brother Chaim, who was eight, died of frostbite and hunger during the winter of 1944. One morning he was just dead. Cold and stiff. We dug his grave and buried him at the top of the hilltop.

Towards the end of 1944 we saw the Soviet Air Force and Polish Air Force planes flying over us from east to west. Then the thud of bombs, falling on German positions. The Luftwaffe had always flown west to east. There was antiaircraft fire at the Soviet planes at first. After the bombing runs the antiaircraft guns fell silent.

In the spring of 1945, after weeks of no bombs, when the Polish farmers came into their fields, we understood the war was over.

Then we walked back to Biezun, where we had lived. But no one from our old life was still alive in that town. The Polish Red Cross was there. And they helped us, first to a displaced person's camp, and then to Canada, where my mother had cousins in Montreal.

As far as we know, all the Jews of Biezun who were still there in 1939 died—some in labor camps, some in Auschwitz, some in the Warsaw Ghetto, and many in the Red Forest. All but us.

Most of Hannah's work was for nothing. She and most of the people she had tried to rescue died at the hands of the Third Reich. Somehow, we survived—my mother, who died at 96 in Toronto, my sister and myself.

I was twelve in 1939. I have had a rich and long life. The world is sometimes a cruel and unfair place. But sometimes it is achingly beautiful.

Hannah Singer was not a nobody.

THE SHABBOS GOY

It was a good gig, even for an atheist. It was steady work. He could ride his bike. It was only in the morning on Saturdays. All he had to do was sit there and open the locked door when people approached. They made him wear a mask, which fogged his glasses on humid days, but the place was air-conditioned so it wasn't a big deal. They didn't care if he took his shoes off, which he did from time to time when his feet got hot. He wore a yarmulka out of respect and would say 'Shabbat Shalom' to people as they came through the door. Almost everyone was pleasant to him and said Shabbat Shalom back, even the people who looked past him as if he didn't exist. The pay was okay. It covered food, and he had a couple of other gigs—in a wine store, walking dogs, and unloading trucks at a supermarket at midnight three nights a week that covered what he needed to cover, so he could take one course at a time and make a little music on the side. Most of the Jews came at about the same time, when one of their services was about to start, so he'd be up and down a lot for thirty or forty minutes at a time. After that he could rest and take his shoes off until stragglers came or until the next service was about to start.

Sometimes Casper wondered why they wanted him there. He wasn't any real security. Maybe the locked door kept out homeless people or neighborhood kids, but almost everyone who came to the door belonged inside, so he never turned anyone away. It wasn't Casper's job to say this one can enter but this one cannot. It was his job to sit there and open the door for anyone who came. If a terrorist or serial killer came, Casper was dead meat. They told him the glass was bulletproof. But there he was, sitting there in the window unarmed, in plain sight like a duck decoy on a lake in the fall. A sitting duck. Literally.

So when a woman on crutches came to the door on one rainy Saturday in May, Casper jumped up and opened the door without thinking. The woman was dark skinned and heavy. She was middle-aged but not old, and she wore a green and blue kerchief. One of her legs was bandaged and she held it bent so it didn't touch the ground. The crutches made a sucking sound, like the sound slow windshield wipers make in a drizzle, when the woman placed those crutches on the grey tile floor. Casper noticed that the bandages on the woman's bad leg were stained yellow and rust red, as if they covered open wounds that were weeping.

"Whew," the woman said. "Thank you, Jesus. I need to sit down."

"Shabbat Shalom," Casper said. "The service is in the foyer today. Not in the main sanctuary."

"You got a chair?" the woman said. "My breath is short and I be sweatin' up a storm. Need to sit down. Just for a little while."

"Sure, sure," Casper said. "I have a chair right here. The one I was sitting on."

Casper turned and pulled his chair forward, kicking his shoes, which he'd taken off, out of the way.

The woman turned so she could sit. She dropped her weight into the chair, groaning. She held her crutches out as she sat and then handed them to Casper, who took them and leaned them against the wall.

"This some kinda church?" the woman said.

"It's a synagogue, Casper said. "For Jewish people."

A knot of people came to the door, a man and a woman and a girl of about ten. They wore dark wet raincoats, and they stamped their feet to get the water off their shoes when they came across the threshold.

"Shabbat Shalom," Casper said.

"Shabbat Shalom," the man said after a pause. He looked at Casper and at the woman sitting in the chair, and then the three people walked past to climb the stairs to the sanctuary.

"I ain't no Jewish," the woman said. "But it sure is good to have me a place to sit down."

"Can I get you a glass of water?" Casper said.

"Much appreciated," the woman said.

"That leg looks pretty rough," Casper said when he returned and handed the woman a paper cup of water.

"It ain't as bad as it looks," the woman said. "I got me scalded from boiling water. Tripped with a kettle. Then fell right down and broke my damned leg. Hurt like the dickens when I done it. Doesn't hurt so much now 'cept the bandage is too damned tight. They don't want me walking on it yet."

An older couple came to the door. The man was bald and had a goatee. The woman was heavy-set. She was pear-shaped and walked with a limp. They were regulars. Casper opened and held the door for them. He said Shabbat Shalom and they said Shabbat Shalom back. They also looked at the woman sitting in the chair and also walked right by.

"When do they change the bandage?" Casper said.

"They is supposed to change it tomorrow," the woman said.

"It's Saturday..." Casper said.

"I know. I know," the woman said." They told me to come to the ER. That's where I be headed. Don't know if I can make it that far though. It's a walk. And I ain't much for walkin' now. Say, you got a fan or something? It be hot as blazes right here. And I be sweatin'."

"I'm not that hot," Casper said. "But if you are uncomfortable, well, let me get you something."

He put his shoes on. You always have to be ready to do what needs to be done. Then he walked up to the office. There will be a pad there, he thought. A pad of yellow-lined paper will do. She can wave that pad back and forth and cool down.

Sure enough, sitting on the desk in front of the office door was a stack of yellow legal pads. He took one and turned. And then he noticed something out of the corner of his eye. It was a red-and-white *Johnson-and-Johnson* first-aid kit, hanging on the wall next to the door. They told him about that kit when he started working in the synagogue. First-aid kit, here. Call 911 for any trouble. There is an emergency button hidden under each desk in case you can't get to a phone in time, though they didn't say in time for what. First-aid kit. Huh, he thought.

Then he heard someone knock. The front door. He had stepped away from it. Someone wanted in. The buzzer in the office went off. They were knocking and now pressing the doorbell to the side of the door.

So he went flying down the stairs, yellow pad of paper in hand.

There was a man in his fifties and a young woman, perhaps eighteen or nineteen, at the door. The man was tall and thin with half-glasses in front of tired eyes, a receding hairline and a strong nose and chin. The young woman looked like a college student. She was also tall and thin, and also had a strong nose and chin, swept-back black hair and dark sad lustrous eyes. She looked like the man only younger, and beautiful where he looked strong and resilient although perhaps worn down by life. They both wore a little pin that had a black ribbon attached to it on their lapels.

"Shabbat shalom," Casper said. "I stepped away for a moment. Sorry to keep you waiting. I should have been here."

"Shabbat shalom," the man said as he and the young woman came through the door. They stamped their feet to shake the water off their shoes.

"Doctor Ben-Levi! What are *you* doing *here?*" said the woman in the chair.

"I go here," the man said. "Shabbat Shalom. This is my daughter. Ayela, this is...."

"Leonora Barros," said the woman in the chair.

"Leonora Barros," the tall man said. "That's some leg you have there."

"Scalded it with boiling water," the woman said. "Then fell down and broke it. Just my luck."

"And you're here..?" the man said.

"Was on my way to the ER. The bandage is too tight. They was going to change it tomorrow. Thought I could go over today. Just stopped here to rest my weary bones," the woman said.

"Well, good to see you," the man said. And he started to climb the stairs to the sanctuary.

"Abba, don't you know how to do dressings?" the young woman said.

"I'm a psychiatrist," the man said, kindly, and he looked at his daughter over his glasses.

"But we did Ema's..." the young woman said.

"This is a synagogue. There aren't bandages here. We'd need bandages, bandage scissors and tape," the man said.

"We actually might have some," Casper said. "Wait. Just open the door for me if somebody comes."

Casper ran up the stairs, and came back down a moment later, carrying the first-aid kit.

More people came to the door and Casper opened it. Before long there were five people clustered around the woman in the chair, some on their knees, first loosening the old, stained gauze on her leg and then cutting it away, putting antibiotic ointment, new gauze, and a new rolled bandage where the old one had been, wrapping it tight enough to hold everything in place, but checking with the woman as they did so to make sure it was not too tight. The woman fanned herself with the yellow legal pad as they worked.

"That's better," The woman said. "Way better. Thank you."

The woman stood on her one good leg. Casper handed her her crutches. She put one crutch under each arm and leaned into them. The suction cups on the end of the crutches made a squishing sound as the rubber collapsed against the tile floor.

The father, daughter and three other people who had come while the dressing was being done stood up together. They watched the woman rock forward. She swung her good leg in front of her and placed her weight on it. Then she lifted her crutches and swung them farther in front of her yet, the suction cups squishing against the floor again as she transferred her weight back onto the crutches.

Casper opened the door. He didn't look behind him. Maybe someone would say he shouldn't have let the woman with crutches in, but it wasn't his job to judge. His job was to be ready when someone came up and then to open the door for them.

"Glad I didn't wait," the woman said, as she walked away. "Glad I came today."

Then the five people climbed the stairs to the sanctuary, going up to pray.

Casper returned to his seat, ready to open the door should anyone approach.

The rain stopped and the sun edged out of the clouds. Beams of light poked through the trees and made the puddles in the street glisten.

What a day!

THE PROTOCOLS OF
THE ELDERS OF ZION

Stanley Moseson shrank when he heard about the demonstrators in the streets of Jerusalem and Tel Aviv. He was never a big man. Five-six at his prime. A hundred and forty-five pounds. Not much in the shoulder department. Not muscled. The flesh hung down from his arms and face like water spilled in a plastic bag and quivered like jelly when he moved from place to place, which he did only with great care, tentatively. The wrinkled suits he wore to work every day always seemed too big for him. His neck swam inside his shirt collars. There were bags under his eyes.

Jewish people demonstrating against one another! Israeli police on horses, chasing demonstrators! Riot police shooting water cannons! Wasn't the trouble with the Palestinians bad enough? Enemies from the outside, the Iranians, the Syrians, Hezbollah and Hamas everywhere. Putin invading Ukraine—Hitler and Stalin, back again, Amalek and Haman back to torment the Jews once more, Petlura and Chmielnicki back from the dead. Only now the

Ukrainians, those Cossacks, those murderers, only now they were the good guys, with a Jewish prime minister, the whole world topsy-turvy. But Jews tormenting one another? These demonstrators, these Israelis—have they no respect?

They call themselves a start-up nation. What ever happened to the People of the Book? What ever happened to study, observance and humility? Who did these people think they were?

He shrank, contracting into himself. Don't they know? he thought. Don't they know what happens to us when they see us? That should we raise our heads, those heads will be cut off?

It was spring now. The daffodils had pushed out of the ground but had not yet bloomed. The robins and the cardinals were back, appearing as if from nowhere, as if their great migrations occurred in the middle of the night. Purim came and went. The sun rose higher in the sky and the days lengthened. Passover was coming.

But Stanley Moseson bowed his head as he walked. They are coming for us, he told himself. We must always be ready to fade into the woodwork. To disappear. Otherwise they will find us all when they come for us again. They will find me when they come for us. They know who I am already. They must know.

He spat on the ground, something his mother did, something he hadn't even thought about in years. To discourage the evil eye, which his mother thought was everywhere in the world. It's back, Stanley thought. Back. The evil eye. It never left. It is always here. And will stay with us forever.

That was when the three people came into Stanley's store, the store where he still worked part-time selling furniture, Social Security not being enough to pay for the nursing home where Ellie was, and because Stanley himself got a little bored being home alone so much with Ellie gone.

Two men and a woman. The woman was alluring—dark tan

skin, blue eyes, big dark eyelashes, dark brown hair with bangs to the middle of her forehead, hair that cascaded over both shoulders in a way that said she was both wild and free. She wore a tight red dress that revealed every curve a woman's body can have but still suggested there was more to her yet, more curves, more heat. Tan boots with stiletto heels and red soles, and an open white fur coat. She sashayed more than walked as she came through the front door with the two men beside her.

One of the men was taller than she was and much taller than Stanley. He had a shaved and oiled head—his white skin glistened under the too bright white-blue fluorescent lights which hissed above them. He stood straight, his shoulders broad like those of a basketball player, under a black leather jacket that reached to his hips.

The other man was of average height and build, about the same height as the woman in her heels. He had brown hair with a receding hairline, glasses and an intent, studious expression. He was wearing blue jeans, a red cowboy shirt with white mother-of-pearl snaps instead of buttons, and a tweed jacket.

Once upon a time, when Stanley owned the store and was in a hurry to build his business, he would have hurried to greet these people, these new customers. Now he waited. People need to breathe. Customers need a moment to look around, to get oriented. Stanley wasn't in such a hurry now to make a sale and beat out the salesmen who worked for him so he didn't have to pay them commission. He wasn't in much of a hurry for anything or anybody. Better to see than be seen.

The three people walked through the sofas and chairs, past the dining room tables and floor lamps, to the back of the store where the mattresses were displayed. They walked among the mattresses for a moment, a dizzying array, one mattress after the next, and saw the poster advertisements for each in bright blue, red, and green type, showing cutaways to illustrate inner springs of different materials and numbers and different kinds of foam.

The woman put her hand on one or two of the mattresses, pressing down to test for firmness. Then she sat on one and tried to bounce on it.

The Protocols of the Elders of Zion is a document written in Russian about 1903, and is a forgery, to the extent that it represents itself as being composed by Jews who themselves represented the Jewish community of Russia. It was composed of parts plagiarized from many documents, some blatantly antisemitic and some from political satires that were turned on their heads. The Protocols appear to be a plan by Jews to conspire and achieve world domination, quite a stretch, when you consider the plight of world Jewry in 1903, when the world Jewish population was no more than 10 million, a population centered in Eastern Europe, in Galicia (now Ukraine—then mostly part of the Austro-Hungarian Empire), Poland, Russia, Germany, and the US but also scattered in tiny communities across North Africa, Yemen, Greece and Turkey, Central Asia, even India and China—a time when the world population was about 2 billion. Then, most Jews in Eastern Europe and around the globe lived in abject poverty, although some, and some communities, were better off. In America, Jews wandered the countryside as peddlers, carrying pots and bolts of cloth to sell to farmer's wives, during a time when most of America farmed. Then those immigrant Jewish peddlers started little dry-goods or furniture stores in the market towns and tiny cities all across the South, the Midwest, and New England, where they lived in tiny communities of fifty or a hundred, the storeowner's family, a doctor, perhaps a dentist, or a lawyer or two, a jeweler or an accountant, the telegraph operator. In a country without pogroms, most of the time, a place that tolerated them, not embraced them. As a world community, Jews were a people without a home, who barely had the means to care for one another, let alone mount an international conspiracy to achieve world domination.

In Russia and Poland, though, the Jewish communities were often semiautonomous, living side-by-side with their neighbors but also often self-governing by way of Jewish community organizations called Kahals. Jewish communities often used a different legal code and legal system, a process which likely made their neighbors suspicious of this people who kept to themselves, spoke languages that the rest of the population didn't understand, were able to read and write when many of their neighbors couldn't and who, though limited to just a few professions and often prevented from owning land, were sometimes able to build businesses and prosper.

These suspicions were too often fanned by local politicians or others, some seeking to divert attention from their own misdeeds, or for reasons of their own, and led to blood libels (matzah, the unleavened bread Jews eat on Passover to commemorate their flight to freedom from the Egypt of three thousand years ago, was said to be made from the blood of murdered Christian children)—and those blood libels too often led to pogroms. Over one hundred thousand Jews were killed in eleven hundred pogroms in Ukraine and Russia between 1918 and 1921 alone.

What is remarkable about the Protocols of the Elders of Zion is how effective this book was at convincing people in Russia and around the world of a conspiracy that just didn't exist. Far from wanting world domination, the Jewish world was made up of people who lived modestly, studied their traditional texts, hoped for little other than to earn a living and to be left alone, and for acceptance and tolerance from their sometimes hostile and occasionally violent Gentile neighbors. In this way, the Protocols were almost a caricature of what Jews were not, and might have been used for entertainment, except too many non-Jews took them seriously, turning hallucination into fiction, and fiction into murder and death. What cruel pathos! It was as if the authors and publishers of these lies put their own fears, evil designs, plots and blood lusts into the mouths of their victims, blaming the victims for the treachery of the perpetrators, a very dangerous game of three-card monte, a cultural and social pattern we see far too often in our own world, as too many of our fellow citizens turn their fears and hallucinations into self-fulfilling prophecies, as they destroy a world of decency and collaboration by acting on what they imagine, instead of valuing the richness of what we, and they, have—and create profit for themselves out of these lies, fabrications, distortions and deceits.

The Protocols were a big lie, a calumny, not the first but certainly not the last, a fiction constructed to cause a stampede, evidence that human beings are forever gullible, forever distractable, inclined to xenophobia and too often to violence, and forever missing the mark. Instead of building a durable democracy, the Russian authors of the Protocols drenched themselves in plots and counterplots, in lies and assassinations, a heritage that led to Lenin and Stalin and Putin, to the deaths of millions of human beings, a heritage that haunts Russia and the world to this day.

"How may I assist you?" Stanley said.

"We got it covered," the tall man said.

"Do all the mattresses come in king size?" the woman said.

"Quality mattresses come in all sizes," Stanley said.

"Is there something larger than king?" the woman said. "We need the largest mattress you have."

Stanley paused. He did not raise his eyebrows. He was certain he did not raise his eyebrows or even smile a little. He was too old for that. No judgment. Or better, no window into what he was thinking. He was a clean slate. You raise your head, you get your head cut off.

"Mattresses only come in standard sizes, I'm afraid," Stanley said. "You could put two kings together, of course."

"There's an idea," the shorter man said. "What's the width of a king size mattress? We'd have to make sure we have enough space in the bedroom."

"76 x 80 inches. 76 is the height. 80 is the width," Stanley said.

"Seventy-six is six-foot-four. You ain't gonna fit, Oleg. Too bad for that," the shorter man said.

"Fuck you," said Oleg, smiling. "I bend. I don't break. As you both know better than anyone."

"Boys, boys, boys," the woman said. "Ain't I a lucky girl to have you both. We can play later. Let's sort this out now."

"Eighty plus eighty is one hundred and sixty. Divided by twelve is thirteen feet four inches. The bedroom is bigger than that," the shorter man said. "Way bigger." He raised his eyebrows.

"I don't like two mattresses," the woman said. "I like it close. Skin to skin. I want to feel your heat."

"Which mattress do you like better?" Stanley said. "Inner spring, memory foam or latex? Pillow top or not?"

They didn't hondle, didn't try to bargain, didn't try to get a better price like people always did in the old days, as if they didn't know there was a ten percent cushion built into the price to allow for that, a cushion that was Stanley's if he could make the sale without a discount. Stanley offered his card after the cashier rang up the sale, a reflex. The woman took it from him and slipped it into her brassiere. They paid cash and walked out arm-in-arm, the woman in the middle. Smooth. Simple. No digs like there used to be after many sales, the asides that one person of a couple would say to the other under his or her breath, the "they got our money again" with "they" meaning "the Jews" and then the other one would say "yeah but we got a good deal. It would have cost us more at JC Penney or Jordan Marsh." No mention of George Soros. They were gone as quickly as they had come, a summer thunderstorm, more lightning than thunder or rain.

They were mostly men in shul that day, on the morning of the day of the first seder, the day Jews call Erev Pesach, mostly little old men like Stanley, men who wore tefillin, strange little black boxes that hung on the foreheads and left arms of the men and some of the few women who were there, held on by leather thongs. Thirty-five or thirty-six men. A woman or two, but mostly men today, at a prayer service that usually attracted a mixed group of ten or eleven, on the days they got lucky. The sun was up, but only barely. Its slanted brilliant yellow light streamed through the windows at the front of the chapel, flecks of dust dancing in the light which made the dark winter just passed trivial, evaporating any memory of cold and dark. Not like the old place, a dark room stuffed under a staircase, where twice as many men used to gather every day, to daven, to pray in a musty room with study tables lining the front, a room lined with books in Hebrew and Aramaic.

But the men came anyway, heeding a call from their ancient past. It was the service for the bahurs, the first-born sons, men who came to pray and then study together for a few minutes, or at least listen to a report and discussion from one of the men or women, telling about the study of a book of Talmud they had just completed, an old formula to avert the need for a day-long fast. The men were commemorating the death of the first-born sons of the Egyptians, an event that was supposed to have occurred thirty-three hundred years before, the tenth plague, which caused Pharaoh to let the people of Israel go after four hundred years of slavery, but even more, they were commemorating the fact that the first born of the Israelites had been spared by God in that plague. Lamb's blood, painted on the doorposts of the houses of the Israelites, the miracle of passing over, when God passed over the houses of the Israelites, as it is said, and the first born of the Israelites were spared. So, these men, looking backward, were thanking God for their own lives, and for the liberation of their people, so many years ago. And we were slaves in Egypt, the words that rang in Stanley's head, strangers in a strange land. Let all who are hungry, let them come and eat with us, and all who are in distress, let them come and celebrate the Passover with us, to worship God and find freedom together.

Stanley came automatically, each year, every spring, and every year, those words from the seder itself would start ringing in his brain, surprising him with the depth of the feelings they provoked, feelings he didn't know he had. It was an old promise to his grandmother, to go each year to the service for the bahurs. He didn't know how much he believed in the literal hand of God, but he came anyway. Perhaps this service commemorated a different truth, he thought. Old men, as he looked around the room. Shriveled, like he was. Not much to look at. Beaten down by the years, by life, by sadness, and by loss. But perhaps, thirty-three hundred years ago, a band of brothers, who rose up together to defend their community, their families, their people, to fight for freedom together. What a silly thought. But if spring can come again and bring new light and new life, anything is possible.

"Can I help you?" Shirley, a gabbai, the woman who organized the services, who called out the pages and kept things running on time, called out, while the rabbi was immersed in the Shmoneh Esrei, the silent prayer and while the others all similarly immersed, standing, bowing or swaying rhythmically with prayer books open before them, murmuring to themselves.

"We're just visiting," a man's voice said, a voice that Stanley somehow recognized. He turned to look.

The two men and the woman who had come together to buy the bed stood in the back of the chapel—the people whose very existence and whose relationship seemed so overwhelming to Stanley that he tried to forget them as soon as they left the store that day. The woman wore the same shaggy white fur coat, but it was buttoned now. She still had the same brown hair cascading over her shoulders and the same blue eyes, and still wore stiletto heels. The tall man with a basketball player's shoulders and a shaved head still stood next to the woman on one side, wearing a bright orange satin yarmulke, the kind they give out at bar-and-bat mitzvahs. The studious looking shorter man stood on the other side of the woman, wearing a woven blue-and-white yarmulke, the kind worn by modern Orthodox men who wear theirs in the street and at business as well as in shul.

Just visiting? Stanley said to himself. Who, just who, do they think they are?

"I'm sorry we have no seats to offer you today," Shirley, the gabbai, said.

"Wait, I'll get folding chairs," said Morty, who sat in the back and always came late.

"No need," said the woman. "We can't stay."

And then they turned and walked out the chapel door.

You can't stay? Stanley said to himself. You never should have come. Have you no sense of propriety? Of decency? And then he went back to murmuring his prayers, his lips saying the words automatically, words his brain and heart had stopped understanding and thinking about more years ago than he could count. In a moment, he forgot about the three people again. He put them back in a distant corner of his brain, a place from which he hoped they'd never emerge.

Two weeks passed. It is amazing how much new growth can occur in two weeks in the spring, how much life force there is in the earth, lying dormant, bottled up by winter, and how it just explodes when the sun rises higher in the sky and the days lengthen, when the light is gold and yellow in the morning, and the sky is bright pink and orange when the sun sets.

Everything bloomed at once. Redbud bloomed, red and purple flowers hidden in the notches of dark spindly trees. There were yellow forsythia flowers everywhere at eye level. The gray-brown trees gave forth pale green leaflets on all their branches. White blossoms covered the cherry trees. First white and yellow daffodils bloomed. Then tulips of all the colors in the rainbow burst open, the blooms enveloped by broad two or four lobed dark green leaves, the flowers thrusting out of the dark earth on straight long green stems, as the air filled with white and yellow pollens, and insects flitted about in the light.

Even Stanley felt the wild freedom of the springtime and allowed himself some liberties. He went out once without a coat. He frittered away time. He sat one evening on a rusted silver-colored metal rocker on the porch of his house, the first floor of a triple decker in Pawtucket, and looked, just looked, at the huge copper birch across the street, at its new leaves dark red and purple, the color of blood.

Even so, he was surprised when his cellphone rang a little later that evening. The junk calls from people selling things rarely came at night.

"Hello," he said, waiting for a recorded voice to give its spiel.

"Mr. Moseson?" a woman's voice said.

"Hello," Stanley said again. He hadn't quite heard what had been said. "Hello? Anyone there?"

"Mr. Moseson? It's Latoya Green. I bought a bed from you a few weeks ago. You gave us your card," the voice said.

"So?" Stanley said.

"I was there with two friends. Perhaps you remember?" the woman said.

"I don't. Lots of people come into the store. Can I help you?" Stanley said. "The bed, the mattress, is okay?"

"The mattress is fine. I was hoping you could give me some advice."

"Ann Landers is for advice. Or Dear Abby. I sell furniture. During business hours. Thank you for calling," Stanley said. And then he hung up.

Two days later the woman walked into Stanley's store. Alone. In jeans and a simple green blouse. She wore a simple tan coat that was open, and black leather boots, but no makeup now, no huge eyelashes and no lipstick. Her brown hair still cascaded over her shoulders and her eyes were still that shocking clear blue. Stanley was talking to a young woman with three children, all old enough to walk, who was asking about dining room furniture.

"I'm from Argentina," the woman with children said, with just the trace of an accent. 'That's why I have an accent." Which Stanley took to mean, I'm not Columbian, Honduran, El Salvadorean, Puerto Rican, Mexican, or Dominican, like the rest of your customers with Spanish accents, who I suspect you don't like. No, I want you to think I'm married to a Brown or RISD professor, that I have lived in London and Paris, so you'll actually pay some attention to me and answer my questions, instead of treating me the way I think you treat all the others, some of who are undocumented, it's true, and many of whom don't speak much English and want to buy on time and won't keep up with their payments so the furniture will end up being repossessed. I get that. I want you to think I am different.

Stanley recognized the woman with the brown hair and blue eyes instantly but he kept talking to the Argentinian woman with the three children, patient as she broke off in mid-sentence to chase and corral one child or the other. That gave Stanley time: he looked like he was busy, but he still had time to think.

The woman with brown hair and blue eyes drifted from section to section, not pausing to look at anything.

Cherry. The Argentinian woman was looking at a cherry table and chairs. Quite elegant. Not as well made as it looked, of course, because nothing is well made any more—everything is made from composites, overlaid with veneers. Stanley knew furniture. This was better than most of the junk in the store. But it wasn't quality nonetheless.

"Do you have a full set in stock?" the woman said. "The table, eight chairs and a sideboard?'

"Six chairs are standard. I'll have to order the other two chairs. When do you need it delivered?" Stanley said.

"What does delivery cost?" the woman said.

"Free delivery if you pick it up at the warehouse. Our premium weekend delivery is $239.99. Our premium weekday delivery is $219.99."

One of the children tugged at the coat of the Argentinian woman.

"Ma-uuum," the child whined.

Stanley ignored the child.

"What day would you like it delivered?" Stanley said.

"Home delivery isn't free? I thought it was free," the woman said. "Let me think about it." She let the child tugging on her coat pull her away and walked toward the door.

Stanley turned his back as the woman walked away. He didn't shrug. Not for customers. Not for anybody. Not anymore. This is a numbers game, he told himself. If enough people come to look, enough people will buy. No need for excitement or disappointment. What will be, will be.

"Mr. Moseson?" a voice said.

The woman with the cascading brown hair and blue eyes hadn't gone away. Stanley turned and looked at her over his glasses.

"It's Oleg. I need help with Oleg. You remember me?"

"No," Stanley said.

71

"Latoya Green," the woman said. "We bought a mattress from you about a month ago."

"So?" Stanley said. "A lot of people buy mattresses. This is a furniture store. The mattress is okay?"

"The mattress is fine," the woman said.

"And I saw you at the synagogue," the woman said.

"People go to shul. It's a free country," Stanley said. "Still. Maybe a little too free, if you ask me."

"And I called you on your cell," the woman said.

"I don't remember. It doesn't matter. Come to the point," Stanley said.

"There is no point. I'm losing Oleg," the woman said. "He's drifting away, drifting into a bunch of crazy beliefs. He thinks the Jews killed Christ, that Democrats are all pedophiles, that the matzahs you eat on Passover are made from the blood of Christian children, that Jews run the banks, Wall Street, and Hollywood, and that Vladimir Putin is God and is preventing the collapse of civilization, that people in the West are about to be replaced by hordes of Muslim robots."

"He wouldn't be the first to believe these things. And he won't be the last," Stanley said.

"But Oleg *matters*," the woman said.

"Matters? For what? For who?" Stanley said. "The world is full of crazy people. Mostly they run around in pickup trucks with flags. Or drive police cars. Or go to football games. Or jump out of airplanes. Or ride motorcycles. Sometimes they run for political office. Only once in a blue moon do they end up in the insane asylum where they belong. When other people start to listen, they'll eventually come to kill us, but we can usually see them coming, and find a way to run and hide. That's the history of the world. *None* of it matters. They come to kill us. We survive. Any questions?"

"I don't want to lose him," the woman said.

"What do you care?" Stanley said. "You've got the other one."

"So you do remember," the woman said.

"I remember everything. What I remember doesn't matter either," Stanley said.

"You're wrong about that," the woman said. "Every person, every act, every word matters. What do you say at Passover? Let all who are hungry, let them come and eat. Let all who are in distress, let them come to be with us. Don't you say a blessing for every meal, for every new fruit of the season, for every moment, thanking God for sustaining you and allowing you to reach each new day?"

"What do you care about what we say? That's our business," Stanley said. "And your Oleg, he's just one more Cossack. A Russian, no?"

"A Russian. A human being."

"Like the human beings invading Ukraine? And killing everything and everyone in sight? Bombing schools and hospitals. That kind of human being?"

"He's here, isn't he? Not bombing anyone."

"So why me? What do you want from me?" Stanley said. "I'm a furniture salesman. Not a psychoanalyst. He needs a different kind of a couch than what I sell."

"He wants to meet you," the woman said.

"He met me!" Stanley said. "We had a very nice conversation. You bought a mattress. It was very nice. Business is business. I have nothing more to offer. Tables. Chairs. Beds. Mattresses. Sofas. That's what I do. I don't do advice."

"Yann told him to talk to you. After seeing you in the synagogue. To talk to a real Jewish person. So he sees you as a human being, not an idea. To understand that you have a rich inner life, like the rest of us."

"Yann?"

"Yann. Our other friend. Who *is* a psychoanalyst."

"Yann is Jewish perhaps? He looks Jewish. But Yann..."

"He's a Buddhist. But he changed his name. From Jacob. Born Jewish. Just not Jewish now."

"What is this world coming to?" Stanley said. "Men who are women. Women who are men. People who sleep three in a bed. Black people who look white. White people who want to be Black. Pretty soon we won't be able to tell left from right. Or up from down. Or day from night. There are ten commandments. Not thirteen or twenty. Not six-hundred-and-thirteen either. Or twelve hundred. Enough is enough!"

"You'll meet Oleg?"

"I'll meet Oleg. But in a public place, not in a dark alley. In broad daylight. With other people around. But understand this: I am Stanley Moseson. A furniture salesman. A schnoorer. Not a rabbi. Not an expert. Not a holocaust survivor. I don't know Torah or Talmud. I can barely read Hebrew. So I am no example of anything for anyone. Just a man, just a typical average human being, and barely that."

They met on Congdon Street, at the Roger Williams Memorial, in the little park that sits on top of Providence and seems to hang over it, where the whole city sits below you, open and palpable like a chessboard where you can see all the pieces and how everything stands in relation to everything else.

It was a cool day in spring. There was no frost anymore. The sun was strong when it rose high in the sky but the sky was often full of clouds, so moments of bright sunlight were few and far between. A stiff wind blew off the port, a wind that made the flags around the memorial flap and crack and the ropes that held them snap against the flagpoles, their hardware ringing on the metal poles. The leaves on the trees were fully formed and open but they were still small and pale green. The daffodils had come and gone—their blooms now tan and withered but their thin foliage abundant and dark green on the ground. The tulips had bloomed but they also were now past their prime, their petals bright red or yellow but open and drooping, flowers bowed over, the yellow pistil, style, and stigma hovering over a black stellate base, broad leaves surrounding each flower like cupped hands trying to bring a mouthful of water, sweet and cool, to someone's mouth,

Stanley was late, of course, because he didn't want to be there. He dreaded talking to three people at once and dreaded talking to these three people even more. He beat himself up as he drove, calling himself a fool for doing this. I have no interest in these people, he told himself. And they certainly had no interest in me. Goyim. Mishegoss. In a world that has gone completely crazy. It's going to be a complete waste of my time.

Oleg sat on a bench just north of the Roger Williams monument, his eyes closed, basking in the sunlight. Stanley sat on the bench next to him, the strong sun illuminating Stanley's face, making his old and withered pink-white skin glisten.

"I didn't think you'd come," Oleg said.

"I didn't really want to," Stanley said. "But here I am."

"Nice day," Oleg said.

"As long as it doesn't rain," Stanley said. "What can I do for you?"

"I don't know," Oleg said. "Meeting you like this wasn't my idea."

"That makes two of us," Stanley said. "They tell me you like Hitler."

"Putin. Also Hitler. But mainly Putin now. The world needs strong leaders."

"Why? So they can blow things up? Everyone dies of something. There's no need to rush and to kill more people before nature does that by itself. God is complicated. People are born. Others die. But he or she or they don't appear to need our help killing people. Everyone dies of something without our help. In due time."

"There is a conspiracy. Without strong leaders, people become confused. Families disintegrate. There is chaos on the street. Muggings. Violence. Mayhem. Murder."

Oleg stood and began to walk off toward the monument. Then he turned and walked back. Then he turned again and walked away, and turned and walked back again, and paced back and forth, back and forth.

"Look mister," Stanley said. "There is no conspiracy. People aren't that smart. I have news for you. Jews aren't that smart either. We fight with each other all the time, just like everyone else. We believe impossible things: burning bushes, oceans that part, wrestling with angels, and people turned into pillars of salt. And we do the same thing over and over again, expecting a different result. You really think that sitting in some synagogue and murmuring the same words over and over has any impact on the world? That old men arguing over old books is doing the world any good? Or that good acts are going to bring the Messiah? Mostly we hallucinate and call our hallucinations holy. At least that keeps us from getting into trouble, at least some of the time. Or used to. But if you want to hate us, go ahead. You wouldn't be the first. Or the last. We survived your Hitler. And we'll be here after your Mr. Putin is long gone. What did Shakespeare say? Sic semper tyrannis? Such is the way of tyrants, to die on the swords they brandish."

"Yann says that these beliefs come from an unconscious fear and repression of my sexuality. That I'm afraid I can't control myself or constrain my desires, and that I'm afraid others have the same impulses, which, if everyone acted on them, would lead to a world of constant tumult, a world of no certainty, a world where nothing can be understood or felt because everything is always changing. He's only part right. That *is* what worries me. But I'm conscious of those impulses and those fears."

"You don't look like someone who is afraid of anything, sonny boy," Stanley said.

"No, you don't understand..." Oleg said, and then he spun around.

There was a huge noise.

A loud farting roar and the trumpeting sound and screech of a hundred unmuffled gas engines, a hundred simultaneous controlled explosions, a barrage, a blast, was coming up the hill from Angell Street.

A pack of all-terrain vehicles, bright and camouflage green, blue, yellow, and red swarmed up the street, darting in and out, popping wheelies as they came on, with a swarm of dirt-bikes, their chromed exhausts swept up and back, their frames lifted so they barely touched the ground, circled in and around the ATVs, the dirt-bikes like flies or gnats swarming around the backs of an elephant herd.

"Watch out," Stanley yelled, as three or four of the dirt bikes jumped the curb and swarmed into the little park, racing up the asphalt footpaths. Stanley stood and then ran to stand behind a tree.

But Oleg, caught in the middle of the footpath, stood his ground.

Two of the dirt-bikes came down the path side-by-side. They turned a corner at the bottom of the park, just below the statue of Roger Williams, and then came right at Oleg, who squared his shoulders and held both hands out in front of him as if he were a traffic cop, ordering the oncoming cars to stop.

The dirt-bikes came straight at Oleg.

"Wait!" Stanley said. "YOU! Stop!" He stepped out from behind the tree. But the dirt-bikes kept coming, bearing down on Oleg.

"ASSHOLES!!" Stanley yelled. It was the loudest he'd ever yelled, more like a bellow than a yell, a great noise that Stanley, who always did his best not to be noticed or seen, didn't know he had inside him.

The dirt-bike riders who had focused on Oleg and were riding right at him turned their heads to the noise and then together shifted in their seats. The dirt-bikes swung toward Stanley, moving as one, like synchronized swimmers or precision pilots flying in formation. The bikers roared onto the grass, so close to Oleg that he could feel their wind and the pressurized air from their exhausts.

Stanley dove behind the tree.

By the time Stanley realized he was on the ground, the bikes had zoomed past him, their riders cat-calling as they went. They found another asphalt path and turned onto it. Then they popped wheelies together and rode out of the park to catch their posse, a final flourish to show who runs the world now, who was wild, who was free, and who was invincible.

Then hands lifted Stanley, who started coughing.

"Mr. Moseson, are you alright?" one voice said.

"Call 911," another voice said.

In a moment, Stanley was sitting on a bench with a knot of people clustered around him.

"No 911," Stanley said. "I'm fine. A little shook up, that's all. They missed."

"What is it with you people?" Oleg said. "Don't you understand the world hates you? I'm starting to hate you. And you still try to save my ass."

"Don't you 'you people' me," Stanley said. "That was me, sonny boy. Nobody else."

"They were going to run me down," Oleg said.

"You don't know that," Stanley said. "They could have swerved at the last minute. They're kids, just trying to show how big they think they are. It's all just bluff."

"I still don't get it," Oleg said.

"Listen, smartass," Stanley said. "There isn't much to get. Life matters. Nothing else. Dead people don't get to change their minds. I couldn't just stand there and watch you get mowed down. Regardless of how crazy you live or how crazy you think."

"This doesn't change anything," Oleg said. "You people are still running the world."

"Nix on the 'you people'," Stanley said. "I told you once already. Don't make me repeat myself. Stupidity runs the world. Greed runs the world. The rest of us, we're just trying to get by, trying to live our lives. In the margins. By not being noticed. That's all there is to it. Stay out of harm's way. Don't raise your head up. Or it will be cut off. Get that memo?"

Rescue pulled up on the street, sirens blaring. At that moment, the woman with the blue eyes and cascading brown hair appeared. She was wearing tight designer blue jeans and a sequined denim jacket. The shorter white man with glasses, the one named Yann, appeared on the other side of Oleg.

"How'd it go?" Yann said, as the people milling about the park pointed at Stanley and Oleg.

Three EMTs in jumpsuits ran up carrying a red go-bag.

The sun burst through the clouds, its brilliant light illuminating everything, the green grass, the Brown and RISD students lying on blankets, the statue of Roger Williams, and the streets, cars, buses and buildings in the city below them, at their feet.

"Want to tell me what happened?" the lead EMT said. "Anybody hurt?"

"I stumbled and fell," Stanley said. "I'm fine."

"What's your date of birth?" the lead EMT said, and then he answered his own question, in his own mind, before Stanley replied. The guy had to be seventy or seventy-five. He needed to be evaluated in the ED. Simple as that.

"I'm fine," Stanley said.

"Why don't you come with us," the lead EMT said. "We'll get you evaluated."

"I'm going home," Stanley said. "Thank you for your interest. I'm sorry for your trouble. But even thirty-five nice people just like you couldn't get me to go to any emergency room. Thirty-six couldn't either."

Stanley stood. He brushed the grass and leaves from his knees and shoulders.

Then he walked away.

THE KADDISHER

He was special because he was his father's kaddisher.

In those days we only counted men in a minyan, in the little group of ten you need to daven, to pray together, to say the most important prayers, although as we all know every prayer is important, each in its own way. He was the only boy in the family, with three sisters. So according to halacha, religious law, only Howard could help make the minyan that is needed to say a proper Kaddish. His sisters could say Kaddish themselves, of course. They could go to shul and say Kaddish in the eleven months that are required after a parent dies, and then once a year, at their father's yahrzeit, the anniversary of their father's death on the Hebrew calendar. But only he, Howard Levitan, could be one of the ten men needed to say Kaddish in a formal, public way, the way that matters most in Jewish tradition, G-d only knows why.

Howard didn't remember when his father told him about being his kaddisher the first time. But he knew about it deep in his soul, as if he had been born knowing it, and he knew that his father was proud of him because of the simple fact of his gender and what that meant in the community. You are my kaddisher, his father would say to him quietly as they walked to shul together on Rosh Hashanah and Yom Kippur while his father thought about his own mortality and his tiny place in this big, complicated world. And then his father would quote a verse from parashat Vayera, in Bereshit, in Genesis. וַיֵּלְכוּ שְׁנֵיהֶם יַחְדָּו Vyalchoo schnehem yachdov. *And they went together, both of them,* the verse that is repeated three times in the story of the binding of Isaac, as Isaac and Abraham go to the place where Abraham plans to sacrifice his only son, his beloved son, following what he thinks is G-d's order to kill his own child, until Isaac is redeemed by an angel.

The text says, *they went **together**,* וַיֵּלְכוּ שְׁנֵיהֶם יַחְדָּו, *both of them,* his father would say. Why does it say "together" *and* "both of them?" Howard's father would ask. It is repetitive. Redundant, yes? No, his father would say, answering his own question. It is repeated for emphasis. The Torah wants you to understand how close Abraham and Isaac were, that they were as one person, father and son, the past and the future, the tree and the fruit of the tree, the seed and its germination, two souls with one destiny. The Torah wants you to understand the depth of Abraham's faith and the intensity of Isaac's love for his father, so you understand what it meant for Abraham not to withhold what he cherished most.

What Howard's father didn't say was what he really meant, which was that he felt that same intense love for his son and wanted to feel, no, wanted to *know* Howard felt that love for him. Howard's father was not a man who ever talked about what he felt. Ever. Only about what he thought he knew, suspected was going on behind his back, or what he was afraid of.

And then the rest of the year, when they walked to shul together on Shabbos, his father would introduce him to any old friends they might meet on the street who were also walking to shul, saying "Louie, I want you to meet my son Howard, my kaddisher," and those men from Russia-Poland, who were bald and wrinkled, with sad eyes but warm smiles, and who all seemed to carry the world on their shoulders, would shake Howard's hand very formally, look him in the eye, and tell him to listen to his father, a learned and good man. This started when Howard was a small child, before he was five years old and so small that these old men towered over him, their legs as big and thick as tree trunks, their bodies blocking the light. Howard was always his father's kaddisher. This was a position of love, honor and trust, and it occupied a central place in Howard's soul.

Years passed. Howard grew up. He moved away for college, from which he dropped out. It was the sixties. He had a wild youth and then he settled down. Married, children of his own, professor, expert in his field, tenure, lectureships, awards, committees, panels and boards, the whole nine yards.

During that time the world changed. The Jewish neighborhoods of the Lower East Side, the Bronx, the Upper West Side, Washington Heights and Brooklyn, small versions of Warsaw in America with their Jewish bakeries, kosher butchers, kosher fishmongers, little department stores, Jewish owned hardware and dry-goods stores, and hundreds of little shuls and shtiebelach (tiny store-front synagogues), completely disappeared. Howard's memories were memories of a lost world, just as his father's world in Warsaw had been lost, swept away by history. The chaos and anarchy of both those worlds, but also their familiarity, riches, and wisdom were gone forever.

Now there were no men with sad eyes and warm smiles to meet walking to shul. People lived in Westchester County, New Jersey, and Long Island. In suburban tract houses and on little estates. They bought big cars which they drove proudly from place to place. No one walked to shul anymore, or almost no one. No one saw their friends from Poland on the street because that generation had died out. That generation's children moved to

Berkeley and New Haven, to Cambridge and Somerville, to LA, Austin, and Seattle. Everything was different. You couldn't tell who was a Jew any more just by looking and listening to them. Names were different. Faces were different. No one spoke with an accent. No one Howard knew spoke Yiddish, and you never heard Yiddish spoken on the street unless you went to Eastern Parkway in Brooklyn, to Monsey in Rockland County, to Bnei Brak outside of Tel Aviv, Mea Shearim in Jerusalem, or to Miami. Everyone had become Americans. Jewish Americans, perhaps. But Americans, just like everyone else.

Howard's parents died. He grieved for them—and said Kaddish, not every day, but at least a few times a week for eleven months, for both his mother and his father. After his year of mourning was over, he made sure he knew the anniversaries of his parents' deaths on the Hebrew calendar so he could say Kaddish on their yahrzeits. He went to the cemetery once a year, sometimes a little more. He was a good son. A dutiful son. He remembered.

But memory alone was also inadequate. The past was past. Lost. Dead. Gone. History, William Faulkner be damned. Even so, nothing he did now and nothing he knew did enough honor to that lost world, to honor its kindness and decency, to honor the love and the gentle holiness that emanated from those old men and women. They were gone, as was natural, but they had taken something incredibly valuable with them. The world of Howard's soul, the warm, familiar world in which people loved, laughed, and listened—that had disappeared with those old men and women. Gone before Howard had even noticed it was there. A mist that had burned off with the morning sun. A dream that Howard couldn't remember after waking.

Before long there would be no minyanim, no places to daven where Howard felt comfortable. No one else missed any of this. No one knew. No one cared. No one else remembered.

It didn't matter. Life goes on. Change is inevitable. Shit happens.

In this certain invisible way, Howard was now completely alone. And living in a world of memories that no one else had. With emotions that no one else felt.

Then one day a letter came in the mail, addressed to his father, forwarded from his father's last address. It was from his father's synagogue in Brookline. A reminder. His father's father's yahrzeit was coming up in three weeks. There was a minyan at 5:45 pm, 7 am and 5:45 pm the following afternoon. It is customary to donate to charity in the name of a loved one, the letter said. Or make a donation to the synagogue itself, or to the Rabbi's tzedakah, or charity, fund.

Strange, Howard thought. He never knew his grandfather, his father's father. In all these years he hadn't ever thought even once about his grandfather's yahrzeit. As a child, he had been to the cemetery where his father's parents were buried a few times. It was somewhere in far distant Queens, in a cemetery plot put together by his grandfather's landsmanshaft, the burial society organized by people from Ciechanow, a city just north and west of Warsaw where Howard's grandfather was born and had grown up. Sometimes, rarely, maybe once or twice, he went to the cemetery with his father on his grandfather or grandmother's yahrzeit, and as a child marveled at the old men from Poland dressed in unpressed dark suits and wrinkled shirts yellowed with age, who lay in wait for anyone who came to visit a grave. Those old men would say El Malei Rach-amim for you so you should give them a dollar or five dollars, which they'd call and you'd call tzedakah, righteous charity, which it probably was, but you and they meant different things by the word tzedakah. Howard knew somehow that those crumpled dollars were all the old men lived on, having found no real place for themselves in America after fleeing Europe just before or, G-d-forbid, just after, the war and the camps.

Howard's father had been *his* father's kaddisher, Howard's

grandfather's kaddisher. But who was there to say Kaddish for Howard's grandfather now, now that Howard's father was gone?

In Howard's attic there was a box. In the box were his father's papers. In his father's papers there was a file marked "family." In the file was a map which showed the location of Howard's grandfather's and grandmother's graves, and a receipt, from 1928, from the Ciechanow Landsmanshaft Burial Society, for eight gravesites. Seventy-five dollars. The receipt was in Yiddish, written in Hebrew characters, so it was written on the page from right to left. There was a rubber stamp on it, in English, that said "Perpetual Care". In 1928 seventy-five dollars was a fortune, especially for a man who had come from Europe only twenty-five years before, had just started a dry-goods store in the wilds of the Bronx, and had three young children.

What was it about men like his grandfather and men of his grandfather's generation, the immigrants, that they bought gravesites before they bought their first houses or cars? What did Howard's grandfather know that Howard didn't know? Or were they all just depressed, just traumatized?

Queens was a three-hour drive. Four and a half with traffic. It wasn't on the other end of the world.

To Howard's amazement, the cemetery wasn't the dark place he remembered from childhood. The main building, a Victorian office structure made of red-brown stone and dark wood, looked like it belonged in a park, not in a cemetery. It had flying buttresses and a slate roof that stretched out over the walls of the building like an umbrella. There was a long rectangular parking lot filled with late model cars which glistened in the mid-afternoon sun, their tinted windshields and windows dark green against the black pavement, so the parking lot looked like the eye of a honeybee, magnified many times. Lots of little lenses. Once a upon a time, Howard thought, the bumpers and door handles of all these cars would have been made of chrome, and the parking lot would have sparkled in the sunlight like a crystal chandelier. But that was long ago and far away.

A funeral cortège pulled in and parked under the portico of the red-brown building. The funeral director hopped out of the lead car, its bumper festooned with a yellow flag held in place by a suction cup. The hearse was behind the lead car and was followed by the long black mourners' limousine, its windows dark, its fenders as long as a football field, glistening and mirror bright. Behind the limousine was a line of cars stretching into the street, each with a small yellow flag attached to the front bumper, each with its headlights on. Sadness for someone, Howard thought. But perhaps this is the funeral of a woman or man who lived a long and productive life filled with happiness and joy, their passing a cause for wistful gratitude about a life well lived, not a time for sadness. Still, Howard thought, one person's life has ended. One small flame has gone out. For that person, the end of consciousness, of both sorrow and joy. Enormous, the end of life. Unimaginable, yet an event that happens millions of times every day. From dust to dust.

It was April. The leaves were not back yet on the trees. The air was still cold and the light thin, but also stronger in the afternoon than it had been a few weeks earlier. There was a chilling wind but the birds were back, and chirping, and the air hinted of the sweet pollens to come, of the green leaves that would soon be unfurled, of the flowers that had broken dormancy and pushed themselves out of the dark earth, the daffodils bright yellow and pale green against the brown beds lining the road near the red-brown building.

The funeral director came out of the building and hopped back into the lead car. The sound of the closing door echoed across the parking lot. Then the funeral cortège drove off slowly into the bowels of the cemetery itself, the cars moving as if they were part of one body, like a freight train or a caterpillar, each car moving independently but obeying the invisible command of some unknown intelligence, so they moved together, as one body, their yellow flags fluttering in the bright cold spring wind.

The people in the cemetery office gave Howard a map to his grandparents' grave. A map on paper. How quaint.

Even so, it took Howard twenty minutes to find his family's cemetery plot. The thin lanes of pavement were named and numbered. The lanes were straight and marked out a perfectly logical grid. A few huge oaks and maples that each looked like they were hundreds of years old pockmarked the acres of headstones, and occasional streams dotted the landscape. Little stone bridges crossed the streams. The few trees had no leaves yet and looked lonely, set against the thin blue sky that was now streaked with gathering clouds.

But the land was otherwise faceless, without landmarks or distinguishing features. Acres and acres of headstones, the inscriptions on them chiseled characters in Hebrew or sometimes in both English and Hebrew. Dark grey and brown granite headstones weathered in the dirty air of New York, many of which had been standing for a hundred years. His own grandfather, who died before Howard was born, was now dead eighty years. Hard to believe that so much time had passed, that Howard could remember stories of living people from another century, even another millennium. But so it was.

Howard got lost three or four times on his way to the graves. But he found the right place at last.

As he drove, Howard remembered the fears and superstitions that children have about cemeteries, and the customs around death and burial, thoughts he hadn't had in fifty years from a part of his memory he didn't know was there. That you have to hold your breath while you drive past a cemetery, because breathing will bring bad luck and cause a close relative to sicken and die. That you are not supposed to step on the actual grave of a person but should walk on the grass to the side of where the coffin lay buried, six feet below. The covering of mirrors after a person dies. The shoveling of dirt by the family, so that the grave is filled before the family leaves the graveside. Things you just don't think about in the normal course of events, but that come rushing back when there is a funeral, or once in a blue moon, when you go to a cemetery on your own.

Howard parked his car. The graves lay in the middle of a field of headstones that stretched as far as the eye could see. This must have been beautiful farmland once, Howard thought. Broad and flat. Acres and acres of it. Could have fed the whole city and perhaps once it did. But there were no farms in New York City now. Not even close. He remembered reading that there are five million people buried in Queens, where the dead now far out-number the living. A recently opened grave sat a few yards away awaiting a new arrival, next to a bright yellow backhoe and a pile of brown dirt covered with bright green fabric to keep the dirt from washing away.

He kicked at the sand-colored dirt with one shoe to dislodge a few stones to leave on the headstones of his grandparents. There were pebbles, but no stones. Generations of mourners had tried the same thing. No stones to be had, not now.

Howard didn't see a soul. He picked his way between head-stones to the place marked on the map. The sun was strong and warm on his head, but the wind made him shiver none the less. A cloud passed under the sun.

"Hey, mist-air! Want to make a misheberach, a blessing?" a voice said in a familiar singsong.

A man walked toward Howard from under a tree. He was walking with the sun behind him, so Howard couldn't really see him in the glare.

"Um, sure," Howard mumbled.

"Make a misheberach?" the voice said again, louder, now only a few feet away.

The voice was of a short, thin man with a long black coat, a wrinkled white shirt and a black suit. The man had payos, the earlocks worn by the ultraorthodox and by Hasidim, but tucked neatly behind his ears. He had pale red hair flecked with gray, a fair complexion and blue grey eyes. His tzitzes, his ritual fringes, were tucked into the pockets of his black trousers instead of hanging loose.

"I, these are the graves of my grandparents," Howard said.

"It is permitted," the man said. "To visit."

"It's a mitzvah, no?" Howard said.

"No. Not a mitzvah. He who mocks the poor offends his maker. The dead cannot make a mitzvah, so we don't tempt them. We leave them to rest in peace. Still, it is understood that you might want to visit. But there is no obligation."

"And the mishaberah?"

"I say psalms. El Malei Rach-amim. Not a mishaberach. But no one who is not observant knows what psalms are any more. You all know the word misheberach, from the singing of that woman. A little clever marketing on my part, no?"

"And Kaddish?" Howard said.

"Do you see a minyan?" the man said. A Jew, Howard reminded himself, answers a question with a question.

"Am I permitted to say Kaddish for my grandparents?" Howard said.

"Am I permitted to go for a walk on Shabbos?" the man said. "There is no law against it. But no obligation either. When a minyan is present. Ten men. We remember the dead. Respect the dead. But honor the living."

"My father was his father's kaddisher. I am my father's. Doesn't that mean...?"

"It means only that you had grandparents. We leave the dead to sleep in the dust. There is life for every soul in the world to come. Who are we to disturb that?"

The man closed his eyes and began to chant quietly in Hebrew.

"El Malei Rach-amim," the man sang, and sang more for a few moments. Howard knew the words, more or less, from funerals over the years and from the Yizkor service at Yom Kippur he had attended in the few years since his parents died.

The man paused.

"The Hebrew name of your grandfather?" he said.

Howard searched his memory in a kind of panic. He knew the names of his grandparents. Of course he did. But the Hebrew names? The names were right in front of him, written in Hebrew on the tombstones. But could he sound them out, right there and then, while this man was waiting for a response?

"Okay. The English names of your grandparents?" the man said.

"Herman," Howard said. He was named for his grandfather who died before he was born. "And Hannah. Levitan"

"Then Chaim," the man said, looking at the tombstone. "And Hannah," he said, with a little emphasis, that said, are you awake or asleep? You don't know a Hebrew name when you hear one? Howard's own Hebrew name was Chaim. After his grandfather. How could he have not remembered *that*? But his brain just didn't work that fast.

The man chanted his grandfather's name Chaim Levitan in a Hebrew singsong and sang a few more lines. Then he began again with El Malei Rach-amim, this time adding his grandmother's name. I could have done that, Howard thought. Wouldn't have been able to read the psalms, though, after the man finished the chant for his grandmother and launched into more chanting.

"You're not going to bug me about laying tefillin today, are you?" Howard said. Then, as the man finished, Howard reached for his wallet. What is the right amount to give a character like this? Howard wondered. I know how to tip a cabbie or at a restaurant. But one of these old guys?

"I'm a Jew, not a Lubavitcher," the man said. "Put your money away. Give to charity. Feed the hungry. Care for the widow."

"I'm very confused." Howard said.

"Confused about what?" the man said.

"I... You... Aren't you here to..." Howard said.

"You think I'm asking for charity? For a handout? Mister, ah, Levitan, those old men died off forty years ago. Fifty. I'm in from Calgary. That's Alberta. Alberta, Canada. So when I'm in New York I come to visit. My parents. Your grandparents were from Ciechanow? We are cousins. Brothers, almost"

"You are...?" Howard said.

"Schapiro, not Levitan. But also Chaim," the man said.

"I'm still confused," Howard said. "Why did you...?"

"I practice Judaism for a living," Chaim Schapiro said. "The head of school in the Yeshiva of Calgary. You looked a little lost. And me, maybe a little lonely. Not very many people come here anymore. Not many people remember. So we stand together for a moment. Two men, not ten. Maybe for a little while we remember together."

"Your parents?" Howard said.

"Are here. Just them. And you?" Chaim Schapiro said.

"Grandparents," Howard said. "My parents are in Brookline, Massachusetts, where I grew up. Probably some great aunts and uncles are here, but most of them were lost... I don't know. I haven't been here since I was a kid."

"My grandparents, also, in Europe. Both sides. Aunts and uncles too. My parents were the only survivors. Lucky, in that way. But also a little lonely," Chaim Schapiro said.

"Lucky they had you," Howard said. "To love and remember them."

"All I have left of them now is this," Chaim Schapiro said. He held his hands out to the cemetery, to the gravestones around them "and Kaddish at Yahrzeits and Yiskor. But I have a full life and five children, and many blessings, Baruch Hashem."

"Also a kaddisher!" Howard said.

Chaim Schapiro nodded. Then he teared up.

The sky had darkened while they were talking. The wind had picked up and was suddenly colder. The sky was a deep metallic gray, particular to New York before a rain, muddy and harsh at the same time because there are not enough trees to block the wind, but only buildings and water towers. They heard the rush of cars and trucks from the highways that surrounded the cemetery, now louder than the wind, noticeable because they weren't talking, a ceaseless grinding thrum, harsher than a river and much more mechanical. The air smelled of diesel exhaust and lubricating oil, and of the dank earth from a recently opened grave nearby.

A little rain began to fall. Then it fell harder, slanted and cold, driven by the wind.

"You have a car?" Howard said.

"Uber from the airport," Chaim Schapiro said.

"Come with me, then," Howard said, as he lifted the collar of his coat against the wind. "Let me give you a lift."

"Kind of you," Chaim Schapiro said. "Let's hurry before we get drenched."

They walked quickly toward Howard's car, Howard leading the way.

וַיֵּלְכוּ שְׁנֵיהֶם יַחְדָּו Vyalchoo schnehem yachdov.

They went together, both of them.

THE WHITE DONKEY

"They say the Messiah will come on a white donkey, riding through the Golden Gate," said Shulamit, who was sitting on the edge of Jennifer's bed.

"Not likely now," said Sammy Li, Jennifer's brother-in-law, who was sitting on a broad windowsill next to a bed tray and an IV pole. "The Arabs sealed the Golden Gate a thousand years ago and put a cemetery in front of it. It's tameh—unholy ground. The Messiah can't walk on it, or, if he does, he's not the Messiah."

"What do you know from tameh? The Israelis are bombing the daylights out of Gaza again. Talk about unholy ground. The Messiah is probably out looking for a different planet," said Jennifer, whose skin was orange.

She looked at Sammy. "Heard anything from Diane?"

Sammy Li looked out the window, where next to the highways, buildings, cars, and trucks, was the muddy green-brown band called the Woonasquatucket River.

"The Messiah will come on a white donkey, riding through the Golden Gate," Sammy said, and waved his hand beneath the

IV pole as if to fan smoke out of a room with a fireplace where someone had forgotten to open the flue.

It was not what she thought it would be.

The air was better though. Diane was up before dawn. The air was as clear as water at five degrees but a thousand times sharper, sharp enough to make Diane's skin tighten and her eyes burn. She could see the silhouette of Monadnock as she walked out to the body-burner, the huge outdoor wood furnace, as the thin red dawn showed behind the bold dark mountain, her skin pulled tight and her eyes and nose running from the cold.

The prick had not even left anything cut and split. There were four footers, and they'd burn, but they weighed about a hundred pounds each, and the damn wood furnace took eight of them. She barely weighed a hundred pounds herself.

The first four-footer wouldn't budge. It was iced in, like the second and the third, so she looked around, found the nine-pound maul with the yellow handle, and swung it, so it hit the woodpile sideways. The first log jumped a fraction of an inch, enough to prove it was loose. Thank God the logs at the top were birch and ash. Birch burns fast, but at least it burns hot and is not as heavy as maple or locust.

It was *never* what she thought it would be.

She dragged the logs across the cement pad, one by one. She opened the door of the wood boiler. A thick cloud of acid smoke sprang out at her and grabbed her, smoke that smelled like spilled gasoline, smoke that burned her eyes and filled her lungs before she remembered to breathe out, not in.

They wanted what they wanted, and never did what they said they'd do, or were what they hinted they were. Every single man after Sammy, who was as dull as wood and afraid of his own shadow. One bad choice after the next. This one the worst. She was done. She didn't have anything left to give.

The last log was maple, and probably twice her weight. She put her arms around it and pulled with all her might.

The log didn't budge. Instead, Diane stumbled and fell backward into the barn, landing on a tarp that covered something hard and cold.

The tarp pulled away as she pulled herself up and dusted herself off.

Fifteen minutes later, she was in a green Miata, towing a trailer that had a white motorcycle strapped to it, headed south on snowy backroads, towards the Massachusetts border fifteen miles away.

By midday she was in Maryland, almost a third of the way there.

Diane knew the moment her mother kissed her forehead, the day she married Sammy all those years ago.

It was a mistake. Her marriage was a mistake. She had married the wrong man.

There was no one smarter than Sammy, no one she trusted more.

He read everything. He knew everything. Classical, Brown, and then URI College of Pharmacy, because it was close to home and he could work in the restaurant at night. When they moved to the house in West Greenwich, he learned how to dig postholes two to three feet deep, and to use cedar for the posts, and how to stretch wire. When his sister went to Kenya, and met Ahmed, he started to learn kiswahili. When his brother married Jennifer, and her cousin Shulamit came to live in Providence and go to Johnson and Wales, he learned all sorts of things about Israel, Jews and Judaism. When Danny turned seventeen and started looking at Harleys, he learned how to winterize motorcycles and how to rebuild old bikes.

But he never learned how to look at her, how to listen to her, or how to tell her stories, and he never learned to sweep her off her feet, and throw her on a bed, or a chair, or a couch, and leave her panting, out of breath, and feeling completely whole.

Their kids were the same age.

When Jennifer got the job in Boston, and Diane was working in Warwick, Jennifer would leave both kids with her when Bobby, who was to die on Flight 11 out of Boston on 9/11, was traveling, which was all the time. Jennifer would drop them at six, and pick them up at six. Diane drove all three kids to school.

Their bond—the bond between Jennifer and Diane—was deeper than that. They were married to different men who were the same man. One heavy and one thin. One outgoing and one too quiet. One successful and one, well, always just home at five. Both kids from a row house in Elmwood. Both Classical and Brown. Both always ready to work at the restaurant on a Friday or Saturday night. Neither one ever looked at you.

So Diane and Jennifer learned to look at each other.

Diane had been gone a year when Jennifer got sick, and it was hard to know what to do. They had all written her off. Diane leaving like that, leaving her husband and her son, that was not something Sammy's family understood.

In the beginning, after Sammy told her about Jennifer, Diane called Jennifer's house a few times because she had to, hoping no one would pick up. She called in the middle of the day. She let the phone ring four times, and then hung up. She didn't want to talk to the kids, who were at school anyway by then, and wouldn't know what to say to her, this errant aunt, this black sheep, who had done what was unthinkable. And she couldn't yet talk to Jennifer. She was somehow too ashamed.

She wrote Jennifer a card. That was all she had in her by then, all she could manage. Just a card.

If she was ashamed before, she was a hundred times more ashamed when Sammy told her about the operation, and the yellow skin, and then the diagnosis, and that awful number. All without her being there with Jennifer, where she belonged. Nine months. Like pregnancy. Only different. So different. So fucking different.

Jennifer hadn't known. Bobby hadn't known.

Danny knew. He was always awake when she finally came home.

And Sammy knew. But he didn't have the words. He didn't even have the thoughts.

Maybe, just maybe, if he'd tried to stop her, she would have stopped.

But no one stopped her. So she was always alone.

It was an old white Honda with rusted pipes, a 305 dream. Rusted pipes, yes. Chunky tank, square as a bank vault, and, at the same time, as thin and light as a stand of young birch trees, bent double by the snow. Those swept-back fenders made you feel the wind in your hair, even when you weren't moving.

"Ten days" the asshole said.

"Do it in a week," Diane said. "Make it perfect."

"Perfection takes time. *You* can make me hurry, though."

"Do it in a week," she said, cutting him off, not the least bit tempted, despite the grease up to his elbows and the slate grey eyes—well, all that just didn't matter now. They were all worthless, every single one.

"I've got a lot of ground to cover between then and now. Make it perfect. I'll be back in a week." She had a room at $29.99 a night, a block off the beach. She could sit on the beach for a week, or even two, but he didn't know that.

"Perfect. I'll be back Tuesday."

And then she was gone.

They looked away when she came into the room but she came in anyway. The two kids were there, and they couldn't stand to look at their aunt. Mamma Li was there as well.

Diane imagined what Jennifer would look like but nothing that she had imagined prepared her for the truth. The air was sweet, like maple syrup. Jennifer was unrecognizable—sunken eyes, shriveled skin, flat hair that had lost its color, no makeup, orange skin that no makeup would fix. Diane started to look away herself, embarrassed at the sight, but didn't, because she was stronger than that, now, once she and Jennifer looked at each other. Jennifer smiled, carefully and weakly. It was a sly smile, and it was a certain smile that she hadn't found in herself for over a year.

"You're back," Jennifer said.

"You're sick," Diane said.

"Sick as shit," Jennifer said.

"Sit up, "Diane said. "I'm getting you a sponge bath. I may be good for nothing, but I'm still a damn-ass good nurse."

And that was how Diane came home. The white Honda 305 Dream appeared in the garage in West Greenwich. Diane found a little place near the cove in Gaspee, where she could walk on the beach every day and watch the waves come in and go out. Jennifer died two weeks later, but not before she and Diane looked at one another, and told each other the truth about their lives.

Two days before she died, Jennifer was sleeping with morphine, and Diane was sitting, watching junk TV and staring out the window, wondering how it had all happened, how she came to be who and where she was, and where it all came from. She had been talking to Danny every night. Danny lived in Seattle now, as far away from her and Sammy and the wreckage of their old life as he could get. He worked the night shift in a nuclear power plant because he, like Diane, couldn't sleep anyway. Danny talked to her now despite himself, but his voice, when he talked, was a hundred miles away, and the real Danny was now hidden from her, perhaps forever. All she could remember was holding him, when he was a little boy, and stroking his hair while he fell asleep, a time that had vanished, like smoke, a time that had, perhaps, never been real.

Jennifer woke with a start, her eyes out of focus and her face tight, as if she were about to scream. Then she saw Diane.

"It was a dream," Jennifer said. "It was like Shulamit said, but totally different. He was a thin brown man with long hair and a full beard, and he was wearing white robes. But he was riding a white *motorcycle*. He rode up the road from Bethlehem, his hair flying in the wind, his robes sparkling and dancing in the sun. When the road dipped to go into Jerusalem, near the train station on Zion Hill, he didn't dip. The motorcycle just kept flying into the air. We were all there—you and Bobby, Megan and Shawn, Sammy and Danny and Shulamit, Suzanne and Ahmed and the twins, Mamma and Pappa Li, my parents and all my cousins, even the old ladies from Romania who used to live in Arad, and everyone's parents and cousins and friends. He circled in the air, the sun dancing in his flying hair and white robes. Everyone reached into the air together, as if we were all holding him up, holding him up together. And then the stones fell away from the Golden Gate. He flew through the gate, into the Old City, hit the gas, and the bike rose into the sky. He circled the city once and then he flew away into the East and we never saw him again."

Diane got a cool wet cloth, and placed it on Jennifer's forehead, as Jennifer closed her eyes, and squeezed Diane's hand, looking straight into her eyes.

"It's not fair," Diane said, as she swept a few loose hairs from in front of Jennifer's face and tucked them behind her ears.

"It's all we have," Jennifer said, and she put her arms around her sister-in-law, and held her, as if Diane were her only child, until she fell asleep.

It was March. The sun had become strong again. It burned through the clouds that hung over College Hill as it dropped in the sky. The city of Providence became red and golden for a moment.

Then the sun set.

FEAR ITSELF,
THE RAPTURE, AND
THE SWEET BYE-AND-BYE

When the news of the Omicron variant spread around the globe, Shulamit Jablowski told her lover Ahmed to stay in France. Ahmed was from Côte d'Ivoire. Shulamit lived in Providence, Rhode Island, in a second story walk-up on Broadway near Parade Street and was in a new relationship with a woman she'd met on Facebook, a woman she wasn't sure was even real. But she didn't want to break Ahmed's heart again. I shouldn't have slept with him, Shulamit told herself. I was indulging his fantasies about a big relationship and did not stay centered on what moves me. It was his voice I was hearing, not my own. I'm not so sure I want a relationship at all, she thought. A good orgasm once in a while is okay. Even necessary. But people are complicated and get needy. I have my own needs and my own desires, Shulamit thought. I just want my space. My freedom to be who I am.

But what was she going to do with the kid? River was seven and in public school. It was a little claustrophobic in their one-bedroom apartment stuffed with house plants during the first lock-down, but they made it work. You invent, experiment, and improvise. Think on your feet. Life became exhilarating. Quiet but filled with new kinds of meaning. New ideas. New emotions. New textures.

That distance learning wasn't much of anything, for kids, so Shulamit took to reading to River at night for two or three hours at a time, reading anything Shulamit herself was interested in: Shakespeare's juicier plays, Foucault, Habermas, the Old Testament (in English but with lines and phrases in Hebrew when Shulamit herself couldn't make sense of what was going on or when River had a question), Clarice Lispector (in translation, not in Portuguese), that George Saunders novel about Lincoln until River just couldn't follow it, and *The Secret Life of Trees*.

Still, the lockdowns were easier on a kid like River than their chaotic life before the lockdowns. No more being parked different places when Shulamit had to go out. No endless choices between alternatives that didn't matter, hair colors and genders and so forth. No more teasing about having skinny arms or a fish face. River stayed home, read books that were too old for her, went for walks with Shulamit to different parts of the city or tagged along when Shulamit went to their garden plot in the spring and summer. Then River rode her bike around and around the community garden, waving to the people who hoed or weeded.

But then they opened the schools again and life for River went back to crazy—in-person learning but everyone had to wear a mask and sit first six feet and then three feet apart and no one could eat in the lunchroom. And everyone was supposed to get tested once a week. Though no one checked so most kids didn't get tested, and for a while no one was sick and then everyone was sick but only with a runny nose or a cold so who really cared. Except everyone cared. And was completely phobic about sneezing or coughing or hugging or touching. And then they'd have virtual learning a day or two a week, sometimes without warning, so no one could plan anything, and Shulamit couldn't organize her life. Or sometimes her class or the school would shut down for a week or two. For this disease that really wasn't making anyone sick. Except when it did.

Then Shulamit started going out again. Which meant parking River different places from time to time.

That was life without lockdown. Which wasn't life either.

Will they close the schools again with this Omicron? Shulamit asked herself. Will Omicron do for them what Shulamit couldn't do for them herself? Which is to have a life that is simple and sweet, but also alive and meaningful.

It is a cool, rainy December. The earth is washed of color. People hurry when they go from place to place, afraid that their eyes might meet those of someone they know and that then they would have to calculate the risks of a fist-bump, handshake, or embrace, understanding that there is no right answer. Spring and summer were impossible to imagine. This drabness is their life.

One rainy Thursday at about six in the evening when it is already dark someone pounds on their door. The doorbell rings, shrill and electric. Then that someone pounds on their door again, and Shulamit walks down the creaky narrow stairway to see who is there.

"Hey," Yudi says, their eyes cool and blazing, but they are looking worse for wear, their face drawn and grey in the fluorescent porch light, their beard and moustache shaved and scraggly now where it had been full, hennaed, chestnut brown, and down to their chest the last time they'd blown through town. Their hair is thinning now but hand cut-shaggy and also hennaed, although some of the henna has washed out so it looks sandy-grey instead of the dirty blond of their youth. The henna on their hands has been mostly washed off. Their face is bruised.

"Makarah motek (what's up, babe)," Shulamit says back.

Then River comes bounding down the stairs, taking three steps at a time, mostly flying, and Yudi grabs River and twirls her end over end like she is a baton. They put her on their head and rub her belly with the top of their noggin like they used to do when she was two and three, and she squeals with delight again like she does only when Yudi shows. Shulamit herself can't stop grinning and something pulls at her from the inside, and she remembers what she saw in him and them in the first place.

"You're ok?" Shulamit says. There is a healing bruise and a scrape on one side of their face and a big healing abrasion on one shoulder, on the same side, and the cloth on one leg of their black tights all torn up on the same side. New black stick-and-poke tat on Yudi's neck.

"B'seder (It's all good)," Yudi says. They speak in English to one another now, mostly. They think in English now. It is a business language, cut and dried, not brusque and poetic the way Hebrew is, with none of the blunt sex or wind of the roots blowing through the speech of their youth. They are who they have become. Still scarred inside and scared to death. But tough as nails outside, to anyone else, an exoskeleton like an insect, a coat of armor for the world to see. Don't you step on me.

"You're not okay," Shulamit says, raising her eyebrows a little. If she wore glasses, she'd be looking over her glasses at them. They see her looking at the bruises.

"Christ hasn't come back yet," Yudi says.

"You noticed? Yeshua ben Josef the rock star? He wasn't so good for the Jews. Wasn't once enough? If we do the same thing over and over, you think we'll get a different result?" Shulamit says.

"The end of days is coming. He is coming back and then the faithful will be lifted..."

"Into the clouds," continues Shulamit, interrupting, her voice clipped and tired. "And the dead will rise and meet the Lord in the air and then the Kingdom of God will reign over the earth. I know the drill. So what else is new? If human beings gave the same thought and energy to one another that they give to Jesus, Buddha, the Hindu gods and goddesses and Mohammed, maybe. But not in my lifetime and not in yours. We are all the same people we were. Humans chase gods and one another. The more things change the more they stay the same. You had a bad fall?"

"It wasn't a fall. It's all good," Yudi says. "You have coffee?"

But when Yudi puts River back down on the floor to stand on her own two feet and drops their pack on the kitchen floor, Shulamit begins to think they might be in for trouble.

The pack itself is orange but dirty from life on the road, so gray-brown orange. Yudi has a tent lashed to the pack-frame. It is blue and gray but it is also dirty so gray-brown blue and gray, with the gray-brown orange of the pack and the grey-brown blue-green of the tent somehow color-coordinated, and there is a light green sleeping pad rolled up and lashed to the pack frame as well, its patina the same grey-brown, so it looks like part of a set; and a very high tech skateboard painted dayglow colors with all sorts of decals also lashed onto the pack-frame. The uniform of anarcho-syndicalism. We are the revolution we make but we need our tools. Shulamit was betting that there is an iPhone what—10? 11? even 13?—secreted away in Yudi's cool retro belt-pack, although Yudi probably picked the phone up used so it is probably hot, stolen in NYC or LA and wiped clean by the brothers and sisters of the street, who do that kind of work. Those sisters and brothers trick iPhones into working like burner phones so they can't be traced, and Yudi knew how to stash or trade their phone out every few weeks so they stay completely off grid. Or mostly completely off grid. As long as they wanted to be.

The pack etcetera on the kitchen floor means that the pack etcetera is not on another kitchen floor someplace in Providence, Pawtucket, Cranston, West Warwick, Central Falls or any other place in the universe. Yudi isn't covering their bets again, this time. Yet. It looks like maybe they are planning to hang with Shulamit and River for a while, to the extent they ever plan anything at all, and maybe they are going to ride out Omicron with Shulamit and River, regardless, as usual, of what their plans are, by which Shulamit meant Shulamit's plans. To the extent Shulamit ever plans anything herself.

But it was okay. B'seder. Maybe Yudi was feeling a need for something more. They come and go like always. Maybe he comes and goes now like always, again, just a little bit. We'll see about that, Shulamit thought. But in the meanwhile, for a few minutes, maybe it was okay that River had her dad.

"A fall running for a train," Yudi says.

"You're okay?" Shulamit says.

"I'm okay. More later," Yudi says.

"Tell now," River says. "I want to hear too." She's insightful, that kid. Who knew?

"You need a place to crash?" Shulamit says, still the master of the segue.

"Stay Yudi, stay. Please....." River says, whining again but taking Shuli's bait.

"A couch is good. A few days. This Covid thing...."

'You're vaxxed, yes?" Shulamit says.

"Are you crazy?" Yudi says. "The ego is a disaster. The self is a myth. The vaccine companies own the world and profit from the misfortunes of others. Let nature take its course. I for one am ready to ascend to heaven, to make the big aliyah, to rise into the sky for my free trip to the promised land, all expenses paid. You fell for their propaganda?"

"Yudi, we are vaxxed and we mask. It's the only right thing. People are dying..."

"I can't stay then?" Yudi says.

"Please Shuli. Pleeeaaasssse...." River says. She knows how to think but she also knows how to whine. A kid. This kidness. A powerful force in human nature.

"We don't hang with people who don't mask and vax," Shulamit says.

"Momma!" River says, as her whine begins to twist into a sob.

"We have a rule," Shulamit says.

"Momma!" River shouts, now demanding.

Shulamit waits a moment for the echoes of River's shout to fade, to think.

"But for you we make an exception," Shulamit says at last, and River's whine turns suddenly into a giggle, as she comes over and hugs Shulamit's waist for a moment, and then goes over to Yudi's pack, which she tries to lift but only knocks over. "A couple of days. On the couch."

"The whole story later then." Yudi said.

"Baruch haba (blessed is he who comes)" Shulamit says, and thinks, River is happy now and focused only on Yudi, which is good.

They climb the narrow staircase, River leading the way, Yudi following with the pack slung over one shoulder, and Shulamit bringing up the rear, the old and narrow stairs creaking and the light from the window on the staircase weak and grey but enough to light their path. Ascending. Aliyah of a sort. A little. One step at a time.

They don't talk later. Yudi unrolls his/their bedroll on the couch. B'seder.

Then the Covid numbers go through the roof, and we get that fake shut down, the non-shutdown shutdown. The Governor won't close the schools and there are still super-spreader events, aka basketball games with 30,000 people at the Dunk, but every reasonable person knows to mask up, stay home, and get themselves boosted. Only the world isn't filled with reasonable people.

So River makes it to Christmas vacation, barely, because kids and teachers are getting sick left and right while we pretend that nothing is happening so that people will still go to shop for presents and eat in bars and restaurants because the business of Rhode Island and of America is business, and we always put what matters most, which is the almighty dollar, first.

Then people start dying like flies again, ten, fifteen, twenty a day, but somehow no one notices and the politicians just keep doing their thing because the smart money really is smart, they know which side of the bread the butter is on, and they know everybody is glued to their screens and phones and other drugs of choice and won't remember any of this past next Monday, to the extent they are going to ever remember anything at all. Shulamit sees and thinks about all this.

Putin gets ready to invade the Ukraine. He's got us figured coming and going, Shulamit thinks. I'm betting he's playing the futures market and is making a bundle every time he moves a tank or an airplane from here to there. The CIA and NSA flip out each time which makes the Dow drop 500 points one day, only to recover the next. Talk about insider trading! He's making the US and all of Europe flip out and he's laughing all the way to the bank. Only I'm hoping that those so-called smart guys in the Pentagon and Mossad have fired up the Jewish space lasers and have them focused on the mud in the Ukraine and are keeping it muddy, not frozen, so Putin can't invade, or, taking a page from Parasha Beshelach when Moshe leads the people through the Sea of Reeds at low tide and the stupid generals of Pharaoh's army who think they are invincible, come after those Hebrews in their chariots so they all drown—horses, chariots, generals, lieutenants and cavalry, the whole kit-and-caboodle, when the tide comes back. Maybe Putin's generals will also get caught in Ukraine and will get swept away by the tide. The more things change the more they stay the same. Go Jewish space lasers! Go Zelensky! And take that, Vladimir! We got us a Jewish President in the Ukraine and yes we do control the banks and the media. We can see you and your lap dog the orange-haired Fuhrer of the Fourth Reich coming a hundred light years out. Don't you mess with us! Is it good for the Jews? We are a stiff-necked people uber alles, but you just can't beat a Yiddishe kupp when we get a groove on.

But before Shulamit had the chance to ingest all that, to sort it out for herself, to make her peace with it or not and move on, the doorbell rings again, a shrill electronic ring, the sound of the bells over the door at Scialo Brothers Bakery on Atwells Avenue only frozen, recorded and amplified so it can wake you whatever the depth of your sleep and send a chill right into your soul even if it were the middle of the summer and 90 degrees.

"I'll get it," Yudi says.

Yudi is gone a long time. So Shulamit goes downstairs.

There is a skin-head person standing on the sidewalk with Yudi and a chopped-out dayglow green and yellow Harley parked on the street in front of the house, parked at an angle but mostly perpendicular to the curb, its raked front end pointed out, ready to go. The person on the sidewalk is thin like Yudi. They are bald with a shaved head and an unkempt matted beard and lots of piercings—eyebrows, earlobes, lips and nose—and have long black and ballpoint blue tats reaching up the side of their neck, on their arms and across their head. They and Yudi are both smoking cigarettes and gesturing with their hands when Shulamit comes out.

It is cold there, and a gray drizzle is falling as night approaches, so the wet street glimmers. The cars have their headlights lit. That light is reflected in the glistening pavement, which has become a black mirror, in which you can also see the red taillights of cars that pass, the traffic lights as they turn red, yellow, and green, and the neon signs from the stores along the street: Barber. Pizza. Cell Phone. Theatre. Real Estate. Spa.

"I'll go," Yudi says, as Shulamit came out of the house.

"Tricky, man," the other person is saying. "Lots of drama."

"Ed," Yudi says, gesturing with his head. "Ed, Shuli, my kid's ema or baby momma or whatever that I told you about."

"Nice to meet you, Ed," Shulamit says. "You want to come in? It's cold out here, Yudi. You'll catch a cold. Then you'll get pneumonia. Isn't there enough sickness in the world already?"

"I'm okay. We're okay. We just need a few minutes," Yudi says. Ed squints at Yudi.

"Okay. Maybe it's cold. You have coffee?" Yudi says.

They come upstairs.

It was complicated. It always is. Yudi had been with a woman for over a year. They rode the rails together. They were trying to get from Portland, Oregon to Miami, so they could spend the winter camping on a beach. But she slipped as they were running for a train. And fell. And hit her head. And died.

Yudi jumped off the train when he saw her fall. He didn't die though. The woman had come to the U.S. from Armenia as a child. Her mother worked in an industrial laundry. Her father cleaned offices at night. She was a tattoo artist who grew up in Brooklyn and went to the Bronx High School of Science before she left all that behind and connected to this different way of living. Her wake and funeral happened three days after she died. But there was a visitation coming up, where family and friends go together to visit the grave seven days after her burial. Yudi was the last person to see her alive. They want to go.

"I'm going," Yudi says. "How can I not go?"

"Her family is pretty old school," Ed says. "You don't know how they're going to react."

"You've talked to her parents, these people?" Shulamit says. "And explained?"

"I never met them." Yudi says.

"They speak English?" Shulamit says.

Yudi shrugs. Shulamit looks at Ed. He also shrugs.

"I don't know them either," Ed says. "Yo. I was only with Ansel once or twice. She was a dope human though."

"Aysel. Her name was Aysel," Yudi says.

"You don't want any of her people wigging out on you as soon as you show," Ed says.

"I never met them," Yudi says. "They don't know me from Adam."

"But you'll talk to them, right? You'll see them at the cemetery and spill the beans. About how she died. About how you were with her. Their only daughter. Maybe they blame you, man. Then they wig out."

"Aysel died, man," Yudi says. "Those people lost their only daughter, who they must think they lost ten years ago. They need people's love."

"And you? What do you need?" Shulamit says.

"What I need doesn't matter," Yudi says. "What they need matters."

"So you'll go," Shulamit says. "And you will walk up to these people and tell them how sorry you are, what a beautiful being their daughter was, and how your heart is breaking too."

"That's crazy, man," Ed says. "And right. But hard."

"I'm going," Yudi says. "Simple as that. The truth is the truth."

"You will take Yudi, Ed. And be there," Shulamit says. "And we will be here when Yudi comes home."

They go off on Ed's bike.

It is late, like ten o'clock, when Yudi comes home. They have a key now so they let themselves in. Shulamit hears the door slam closed, the lock click, and then hears Yudi on the staircase, those old wooden steps creaking with their weight, hears the rattle of the metal banister as Yudi puts their hand on it and uses it to haul themselves up the stairs, hears their windbreaker scrape against the wall as they come slowly up the stairs, as if he is a heavy old man who drank too much and doesn't have the strength to climb stairs anymore instead of being a wild young man of the road who files their teeth instead of going to the dentist, and who dreams strange dreams, sees visions, and thinks their actions, beliefs, visions and dreams can bring the second coming of Christ and make the millennium happen, the time and place where the lion lies down with the lamb, hunger and fear vanish, justice reigns, and angels sing in perfect harmony twenty-four seven. The kingdom of G-d on earth, and so forth.

"It was okay?" Shulamit says, as Yudi stamps the snow off their shoes and then takes them off.

"It was sad," Yudi says. "She was young and beautiful. Full of life. An amazing imagination. Many dreams."

"And her parents?" Shulamit says.

"They were okay. Sad too. Very sad. It is hard to lose a child. Impossible."

"They were okay to you?" Shulamit says.

"They hugged me. We all cried. Even Ed cried," Yudi says.

"You want to be left alone?" Shulamit says.

"It's okay. You know people in this country have been riding the rails for a hundred and fifty years?" Yudi says, as they take off their windbreaker and fleece and hang them on the pegs near the door, under the waxy green leaves of a golden pothos plant that Shulamit has trained to grow over the door, its stems and leaves snaking around the room where the walls and ceiling meet. "They started after the American Civil War, when soldiers had to find a way to get home."

"Hobos and tramps. Maybe half a million at once in the 1930s, mostly men looking for work. Men and women who didn't want to be tied down, who wanted to be free and clear more than they wanted three meals a day and a warm bed at night. Freedom. Not three hots and a cot."

"So?" Shulamit says.

"They had an expression" Yudi says. "*The sweet bye-and-bye*. A song, I think. They didn't say goodbye to each other, like English people do. They said only, 'see you in the sweet bye-and-bye.' "

"Shalom, yes? Perhaps le-hit-roat (see you again)?" Shulamit says. "So what?"

"So nothing," Yudi says. "I have been thinking about it, that's all. The sweet bye-and- bye. Where we all see each other again. Where we are all together again. Where heartache and anger doesn't happen, and people aren't afraid and don't fight."

"The Rapture, maybe? None of this is real, you know. The world is more complicated than all that," Shulamit says.

"Not the Rapture," Yudi says. "Different. Here and now. Real. I'm seeing Aysel right now in the sweet bye-and-bye. I see you there. I see River there."

"Hi Yudi," River says. She is standing in the doorway of her room, next to a dusty rubber tree, in a shadow, in a yellow and blue onesie, rubbing her eyes. Her voice is thick from just waking up. She was standing in the shadows, listening, but talks when she hears her name.

"It's the river of life herself!" Yudi says.

They go over to River, lift her very slowly off the ground so she has time to laugh from anticipation itself, and put her belly on their head.

She giggles. And then she laughs from her belly with abandon, as if Yudi has always been with her, and perhaps, always will.

THE STABLE

The man had a lean and hungry look. The light from our campfire caught his bright, haunted eyes. He had a scraggly beard, and his body was covered with animal skins. He stood in the shadows without saying anything, close enough to be seen, but out of harm's way.

"Come and join us, man," said my father, a big-hearted man with a gruff voice who tried to look more fearsome than he was. "Come sit near the fire. Have something to eat!"

My father studied the stranger. The man did not respond.

"The food's good!" my father said. "We won't hurt you. Not, at least, before dinner. I give you my word." My father is not always so welcoming. He must have liked the man's looks.

The man didn't answer.

"See, we eat it!" my father said, shoveling a handful of stew into his mouth. "It's not poison."

Everyone around the fire laughed.

The man remained on the edge of the darkness. Only his lonely eyes moved, darting from person to person.

"Come eat! Come on!" my father said. "Are you a man or a stray dog? Do you have a tongue?

The man took one small step toward us. This one might be trouble, I thought, but in a good way. A mysterious stranger.

For a moment I was afraid my father had insulted the man and there might be trouble. The bad kind.

The young man stopped. He eyed us warily. Some of the men had their hands on their belts, not showing their daggers but ready for anything. We are always ready for anything. And have to be.

"You can pay for your meal if you want. Or trade. Where have you come from?" my father said.

The man still did not respond.

It was a tense moment. My father was a good judge of men and was just as likely to have a stranger killed as entertain him, once he made up his mind. There was something about this one, something desolate but strong. My father saw it and so did I.

"Don't be bashful, friend," my father said. "You're my guest. Looks like you've done some pretty heavy traveling. Have something to eat, get warm, and then tell us where you came from. Tell us what you saw on the way. How's that? We'll trade you dinner for a good story. We like stories here! Stories, news of faraway places, good lies, it doesn't matter. Eat and then talk. Maybe we'll forget this cold wind for a while. But either join us or go back to the hills. No hanging around. We don't allow stray dogs around our camp. Stray men are no better."

To my surprise the man smiled and came forward.

He was younger than he looked at first. When he got closer to the fire, I could see he had bright dark eyes that were both wise and suspicious. Careful eyes. Not angry though. Eyes that had lived and learned.

Soon he was eating cross-legged before the fire.

He ate. He ate with gusto, as though it had been a long time since his last full meal.

But he didn't say anything, not for a long time. I wondered if he spoke our language. He watched us every second as though he was afraid we were trying to trick him. As if he had been tricked before.

We ate and there was laughter. When someone had something to say, there was conversation. Life was never dull in our camp. But finally, full stomachs and the cold night began to take their toll, and we fell silent.

Then the young man began to speak.

He had a soft lisp. He spoke slowly at first, but once he got started, he went on and on without stopping, the way a man who hasn't seen people in a year talks. The way a man who has something to hide talks. There were many things he said that I didn't understand, and many strange people he mentioned I don't think I will ever meet, but I remember what he said even now, like we met only yesterday.

"It was early, and still cool," he began, lisping. "It was early and still cool as we started on our daily walk through the temple gardens to the stable. Pharaoh was silent, even morose. White marble pebbles crunched under our feet. A small bird burst from a sculpted bush and surprised us. Perhaps that bird touched Pharaoh because he smiled.

"'Ah Moses,' he said. 'Don't you get bored on our morning rides? You're just a commoner, it's true, but the blood of Ra flows in *my* veins. That makes me want more. Always more. I'm never satisfied with what I've got. Don't you ever want to break away, to do something big, to shoot the works, to try for the big time? The horses in this stable are nothing, compared to some of the those some of my retainers tell me about. You know about the fire breathing horses of the gods?'"

"I didn't reply. Pharaoh would go off like this from time to time and he doesn't like to be interrupted. Ever. By anyone. The old king, a plain man, was all hopped up.

"Some days old Pharaoh talked himself into believing that garbage about being descended from Ra. On those days he thought whatever he said was as good as prophecy. I was stupid enough, back then, to almost believe it myself. Sort of. Sometimes. That's what growing up in the royal household does to you."

"'Come on, boy,' he said, 'that woman from the bull-rushes, what's her name? must have told you all about the Wing'd Steed, or of the horses with iron hooves and a taste for human flesh, among those wild theories she has, theistically. Even the Italians have legends copped from us.'"

"I half-nod, half-shrug, so he knows I'm paying attention."

"'There are horses that mount the sky, Moses, horses with jeweled wings and unbelievable gaits...'"

"Suddenly the old man broke off, and I see him trembling. I grasped the old man's hand to calm him down. If he keeps up like this, he'll give himself a heart attack and we'll fill that great tomb too soon, descendant of the gods or not, I thought. Blazing eyes don't fit him. He was a paunchy old noble and usually bored, even with the boys they brought for him every night. I'd seen the old guy steaming angry before, but rarely obsessed like this."

"'Damn it,' he shouted, 'I'm a god and I know it. Those nags. They're the same every day. They're asleep on their feet. They don't know how to run. Didn't that woman teach you how to live, boy? How to shoot the works? I'm of the gods. I won't settle for second best.'"

"Pharaoh quieted as we neared the imperial stable. His face looked unusually pale, set against his white robe and morning sun. I worried that all this quivering, this agitation would get the better of him, and he'd do something rash.

That said, I probably knew more about his gods and about the lies he told himself than he did. Home-schooled maybe. But I knew my stuff. Yochebed was a good teacher."

"The sweet smell of manure and oats enfolded us as we entered the great barn door. The wood-and-stone stable was long and brown inside. It smelled sweet like molasses or compost and earth. The best light was at either end, from the two great doors. The stalls opened out of the darkness, one at a time, one stall on either side, as we walked between them."

"Pharoah's horses led a pampered life in peacetime; in times of war they worked like slaves, hauling and charging, and got mauled for their trouble. We heard them chomping on their oats as we walked, and heard them stamp and snort and then quiet, chewing in the darkness. Two fat horse backsides, one on each side, appeared one after the next in the brown light, good strong backsides with strong, proud tails and powerful legs. We'd each choose a horse from those we saw."

"I saw two or three I liked, on the side reserved for Pharoah, but as protocol demanded, I waited for Pharaoh, waited until he found his god-horse."

"For the first few minutes, as we walked down the line, the old man said nothing. I could sense his disappointment. The same old nags, although these were the best horses in all Egypt.

Finally, exasperated and ready to give up, Pharoah stopped to check one beast out, a big black stallion. He stepped into the stall to run his hand over the creature's flank, but he moved too quickly, without enough warning, and upset the horse, who kicked at him, all protocol aside. Pharaoh, always on the alert, stepped out of the way, a politician to the last. Once outside the stall he scowled, 'Bastard. Bastard lowlife.'"

"The old man squinted, eyed those hooves and moved back to the middle of the aisle. No one could ever call the old man reckless. Or brave. He learned caution when he was young, the hard way, and that's why he lasted so long."

"Pharaoh's voice trembled as he started talking again, quietly now, almost whispering."

"'I've heard tell, from that Greek bookie I mentioned, of a young man about your age, who claimed descent from the Greek sun-god, the one who with four-in-hand and chariot pulls the Greek sun across the Greek sky.'"

"The old man paused and looked down his royal nose at me. I'm okay for company. But not exactly the grandson he was hoping for. The lisp. The posture. I'm a reader, not a warrior. Not a public speaker. Kind of shy after all."

"''That young Greek bastard son of old Helios,' Pharaoh continued, 'a handsome lad with real gumption, who wasn't afraid of his own shadow, who didn't just hide behind his mother's skirts, went to his father, the Greek god of the Greek sun, and asked to drive the horses, horses that put all of these to shame, white winged horses bright and wild enough to drag the sun out of its hiding place and then across the sky. And the father, this Greek god of the Greek sun, gives in, says sure, take the horses out for a spin, and off the boy goes, a mere boy behind those four horses that each put a hundred of mine to shame. Remember that Greece pales before the glory that is Egypt, that those horses are shadows of Ra's fire-breathing steeds; that this Greek god is nothing, a pale boy before the power of Ra; and that Greek sun is just a glimmer of starlight besides the powerful flaming scorcher of the Nile.'"

"The old man paused and took a closer look at a roan gelding."

"'But Pharaoh,' I said, being careful. Pharaoh liked me plenty then, perhaps more than any of the sons, who were always plotting, planning, and pretending that they were the one, that they were favored for the throne. But there were limits to what even I could say. I knew those limits well. I was no bureaucrat, but I was also not about taking unnecessary risks. Not yet."

"'Pharaoh, Phaethon rode behind Helios' horses when he was twenty-two, in his prime and fit as a fiddle. His father, a god after all even if a Greek one, blessed him for that ride! But remember how it ended. Those amazing beasts, sensing that there was a lightweight behind them, a novice, an amateur, tore the steel reins from Phaethon's hands, got their heads, and took off across the sky, scorching and freezing the earth in turn. They tossed Phaethon, dumped him headlong into the sea. Ra is greater than Helios, of course, and Ra's steeds are mightier. Greek mythology is a mess and those little cities are nothing compared to ours, their politics chaotic. It is not possible for men to govern themselves. Men require strong leaders and a firm hand on the tiller, a leader who acts without hesitation.'"

"I was showing off my command of mythology, theology and philosophy, and it made Pharaoh laugh."

"'Close, boy,' he said. "Zeus the thunderer smacks the kid with a thunderbolt and sends him flying when Ghea, the Greek earth, gets uptight. You don't burn your mother and get away with it!'

"He laughed again and jostled me. I've done my job, served my function, acted my role, and put the old lecher in a better mood."

"'Come on,' he said. 'Choose a horse. It's time to ride.' He was smiling in the dark, happy to be in a better mood and free of his visions, of his feelings of dread, of failure, of impotence, which must have come from realizing that he was just a man."

"We neared the far door. There weren't many horses left. The strong sun blinded us. The royal stable manager, a Bedouin from the Sinai, knew his master and his master's moods. He anticipated the attacks of angst and disappointment that occasionally washed over his royal majesty, and so he positioned the horses accordingly: temptation first, then disappointment, with the best saved for last."

"The horses of Thrace, the best and strongest of all, were stabled at the far end, on Pharaoh's side, their haunches rising out of the half-light, the air filled with their snorts and whinnying."

"The old man's spirits rose as soon as he saw those fabled battle-bright mounts. Pharaoh slowed and studied each."

"The first of the good lot was the largest and most fiery, an angry bay mare, and Pharaoh always passed her by, not from fear, or so he claimed, but because his station demanded a stallion or a horse of striking color, and the bay, though strong, was equally mean. To my surprise he passed up his favorite mount, a variegated stallion, whose many colors and blazon blue eyes shamed any horse I'd be allowed to ride. Pharaoh passed up horses number three and four, and I started to wonder what was on his mind.

"He drew up behind a yellow gelding, pink-eyed, white-maned and stomping about in his stall. All show. No substance. Old Pharoah must have still been a little down after all. Poor royalty!"

"The yellow horse was throwing up a racket, snorting like a bull elephant and fighting his lead, kicking the stall and squealing. He threatened to tear the stall to splinters. Like Pharoah, that horse must have felt all bottled up inside."

"The old man nodded. Slaves gathered—they had a wild horse to subdue and saddle. The yellow horse didn't give in without a struggle, that's for sure."

Poor Pharaoh. This was the horse most mad to run, and though the old boy was usually afraid, that day he was beset with speed dreams. I wondered what went on last night, and what stew the palace gossips would make of today's choice when they found out what Pharoah rode."

"But there wasn't time for idle speculation.

"Pharaoh looked at me. It was my turn to choose a mount."

"My usual mount was a small swift mare, a sweet dispositioned, loose-footed thing, who could move like the wind when I wanted and who wasn't prone to playing games with me. I knew I could trust her not to leave me on a low-hanging branch or sitting on my backside in the middle of a stream. I was a good enough horseman. That day I had nothing to prove. When you ride with Pharaoh it's important not to outdo him in any way. Quiet horse. Careful rider. Pharoah was such a plain, jealous man. We all had to work at it to be sufficiently subdued."

"But my little mare's stall was empty. Must have pulled up lame, I thought, and looked at the remaining horses on the left hand side, at the mounts reserved for me."

"I like a horse that knows how to move, that is nimble and quick and thinks the way I think, which is a half-mile ahead. The stable was filled with big-boned war-horses. They're okay for a headlong charge on the field of battle, but their gaits are sloppy, the seat jarring, and they are just too ponderous for a morning ride. I backtracked a few steps, hoping I overlooked something good in the darkness, but I saw nothing of interest and walked back toward the big open door."

"How I wished for a break in the row of high rumps. How I wanted to wrap my legs around one of those scruffy desert ponies the Bedouins love to ride."

"But there was nothing. "

"Then, suddenly, just as I was about to give in and call for an ugly roman-nosed bay, I spied to the right, off on Pharoah's side, a break in the great wall of backsides."

"She was also a mare like Pharoah's usual bay, but this one was jet-black, except for a small white circle about her girth. She was small, even slight, her nostrils flaring with each breath. Tied to the back wall, you could still see her intelligent eyes."

"She must hate the barn, I thought. She looked like a horse with a free spirit. All this hubbub—the horses, walls, people, darkness, noise—she's out of her milieu. She had the blazing blue eyes of Pharaoh's favorite horse, but this little horse was lithe, wildly beautiful, and spunky..."

"I looked at Pharaoh cautiously, for I'd be taking a horse reserved for him. He paused, weighing the pros and cons, but then he nodded his approval. She's small, I could see him thinking. She'll be put to shame by my big yellow charger."

"Pharaoh's horse was almost ready. I could see he was getting impatient and wanted me to hurry."

"I always prepared my own mounts, did the grooming, bridling and saddling myself. The slaves are efficient, but uncaring and flustery. They made the horses nervous."

"I spoke to the little black mare and slipped into her stall, laying my palm on her rear. She was well-muscled but tense and calmed a bit as I talked to her."

"I called for the grooming pieces. She watched me out of the corner of her eye. Then I ran a brush over her. Her coat was sleek and unscarred. Slipping under her neck, I brushed her right side, but she backed off and snorted, as if I hurt her. That's strange, I thought. Horses usually quiet when they're being curried. I looked for a cut or a saddle sore that might be sensitive but found nothing. Must be a special phobia, I thought. Horses, like the people who care for them, are plagued by irrational fears. Quick but calm, I stepped out of the stall to receive a saddle from a waiting stable slave."

"Pharaoh was already out in the yard, grave, attentive and standing on a mounting block. He glanced at me, his jaw set, and I could see he was in a hurry. I watched the impatient old man mount the yellow gelded charger. The horse was brought up, prancing and anxious behind its lead and Pharaoh hopped on without a second thought."

"Pharaoh's horse took off at a quick lope before Pharaoh could get his stirrups. The old man bounced like a boulder rolling down a hill, and I thought the horse might pitch him, but he somehow kept his seat, got hold of his stirrups, grabbed the flapping reins, and brought the yellow horse around."

"I had to hurry then, and with the saddle over one arm, I slipped back into the stall with the little black mare."

"The mare stood still when I threw the saddle on her back, which surprised me. I reached down and under to catch the girth and I tightened it around her belly. As I buckled the girth, she snorted and pulled back on her lead."

"'Steady,' I said, and put a hand on her rump again to quiet her. But this time I felt something. When I looked closer, I thought I saw a strange metallic glimmer from her rump, shining in a shaft of sunlight that poked through from the barn door, or at least I thought I did. Strange, I thought.

"The saddle tight, I stepped backward to take a closer look, hurrying because Pharaoh was waiting."

"I ran my hand against the grain of her coat. She shivered and snorted, as if I was touching a sensitive spot."

"Her skin was pale white beneath the sleek black coat. Sewn into the skin were strands of a golden fiber or thread. The skin itself was tinted yellow-gold in some places and silver in other parts, as if the skin had been dyed. Some desert nomad had tattooed his horse. There was an image there, some scene of brilliant splendor, but I couldn't see it clearly because the black coat had grown back over the artistry."

"I was tempted to call Pharaoh, show him what I'd found, and have a slave shave off the hair that had overgrown in the picture so we could see what was depicted, but I held back. Pharoah was in a big hurry. I found the picture. Maybe it was a great secret, one I'd best keep to myself. Omens and prophecies are personal. They're not to be shared with just anyone. Pharoah was likely to say he'd found it himself and spirit the little horse away if the picture turned out to have any significance. Hold your cards close to your chest, Yochebed taught me. Wait. Think. Plan. This time I listened."

"I slipped a halter over the little black horse's head and led her out into the paddock."

"Pharaoh decided he was tired of the riverbank, and soon we were cantering down a palace road toward unbroken stretches of trees. We rode through a forest, horses held in check under the low branches, and soon we were in the foothills. Whenever we came to a clearing or a pasture, Pharaoh laughed at me and my little black mare, spurred his big Thracian charger and galloped off, not to be seen again until I caught him at a wall or another woodland. The black mare, though little, was very quick, and I don't ever give up, so his royal highness was never too far ahead. We'd catch him going into the woods and then blister past, slipping beneath low branches."

"Suddenly one cloud joined with another and then one more and choked off the sun."

"The sky became green-black and then purple. Wind swept through the trees and whistled in the wooden hills. Then lightning flashed across the dark sky, followed by immense, flat, flapping thunder. Some god has moved the evening cloud burst up, I thought, and deigned not to warn his royal majesty. So much for omniscience and the divine rights of kings."

"Our horses tossed their manes and tugged against the reins. I looked about for shelter, but Pharaoh, flying high and always proud of his lineage, accepted the thunder as a challenge, laughed at me, turned the yellow horse loose, and dug his heels into the yellow horse's flanks."

"The big yellow horse needed no encouragement. They galloped away at a dead run, Pharaoh, short, dumpy, and bald, hanging on for dear life, not looking anything like a horseman valiant enough to challenge the elements. "

"But who was I to speak? I rode to a cave I knew of in the cliffs and led the little black mare inside. Better to stay dry and avoid the thunder and lightning after all."

"The little black mare stood quiet at the mouth of the cave. I didn't bother to tie her at first. What I wouldn't have given for some tinder, dry wood, and glowing embers with which to set a fire."

"But the cave was bare. I walked into its depths, bored by the storm, but the cave was too dark to see. I decided not to press my luck by stumbling about in the darkness. I sat on a rock and watched the rain, waiting for the storm god to release us, and thought of valiant Pharaoh, dashing like a foolish peasant in the smacking torrent."

"Then I remembered the tattoo."

"I tied the black to a tree near the mouth of the cave, split a rock to make an edge, and shaved the hair from her rump."

"Soon, whole sections of white, gold and silver skin were bare. In the light of the clearing sky, lit from time to time by flashes of lightning, I saw that the skin was not merely tattooed, nor was it simply dyed, but that gold and silver dyes were used to shade and accent a drawing on the skin that was stitched in fine gold thread, which produced the glitter I saw at first."

"Finally the skin was clear of horsehair. The drawing or scene completely covered one half of the horse's rump."

"What I saw was a mural in miniature, a pastiche, a number of tiny views that told a story, a scene more carefully drawn and more true-to-life than any of the murals that adorn Pharaoh's palaces or the paintings in halls and houses anywhere in Egypt."

"The largest panel was in the center and depicted a multitude, a crowd as numerous as the stars in the heavens, walking through a wilderness, following a gold and silver light that came down from the heavens. Scattered around the main panel were smaller scenes: a tiny boat shaped like a cradle floating in the bull-rushes near a knot of beautiful bathing women; a young boy wandering in a great palace, looking dull and out of place; a murder, where one man, young and strong, strikes another, older and not so fit looking, with a whip, a third man lying at their feet: some vegetation consumed by fire; a panel showing snakes and magicians; and one that showed an oasis in the wilderness, with water flowing from the rocks."

"This wasn't just a flat picture like those drawn by Pharaoh's artisans. This picture had depth and perspective. Everything looked real. "

The young bearded man stopped there.

We were all still awake, and waited for more, but nothing more was forthcoming.

We looked around at one another, waiting for the story to come to some conclusion,

"Well? Isn't there more?" my father said. "Will you just abandon us there? What happened between then and now? What happened to that little mare? Did you make it back in one piece? Did Pharoah? Or is this just a little fairy-tale, a fantasy you concocted, a story made to trade for warmth and eats?"

The bearded man looked up, hurt. He paused, as if thinking, as if he was struggling with himself about how much more to tell.

When he started again, his lisp was more pronounced, the sound of a snake slithering in the sand. He ignored my pa and looked sadly into the fire.

"The storm abated before long. On my way home I caught an overseer beating one of Yochebed's people, leaning heavier than necessary on the lash. My soul, still agitated by that encounter with high art, called for better things, and I told the overseer to let the slave alone. Perhaps he was so angry that he didn't hear me. Perhaps he didn't care who I was or what I said. But it felt to me like disobedience. The slave was suffering. I dismounted, myself enraged, called to the overseer again, and let the reins of the little black horse drop."

"The overseer did not stop beating the man. I shouted with all my might and spooked the little black mare. She kicked up her heels and disappeared."

"Angered both at the idea of having to walk home and by the impudence and cruelty of the overseer, I shouted again. The overseer still did not respond."

"I took a swing at the man. I hit the overseer once, twice, and then he dropped, dead, I discovered. The slave ran off. No doubt he will testify against me."

"I fled on foot after sinking the body in the sand, knowing full well that Pharaoh's men would find him before long."

"Pharaoh's men still pursue me, so I live alone now in the mountains or wander in the desert, waiting till the heat's off. That foreman was the bastard of a wealthy and important family. Pharaoh could not let me go free if he wanted to, and after running off the way I did I dare say he'd like to see me disemboweled."

"Only when the night is cold and my stomach empty do I come towards the firelight, and exchange this story for warmth and a meal, though like you, most who hear the story think it's nothing more than fantasy, the wild hallucination of a loner, a human desert rat."

Not much of an ending, truth be told. Still my father, was somehow smitten with the man by the story and sent me to him, to give him warmth and better.

That man lived and traveled with us for nearly two years. He had a flock of his own, which grew larger the longer he stayed with us.

His seed caught in me twice—one cries before us now, and one is on the way.

But the bearded man went off again not long ago, back to Egypt. He said he had some unfinished business there. He promised to return for the man-child and myself, but you know compulsive wanderers.

When I see him again, I'll believe it.

FROM

RHODE ISLAND STORIES

THE FIRST VIOLINIST
OF LOWDEN STREET

To arrange the audition meant going places Sonia Bloch hadn't been to for a long time, places she never thought she'd go again. But Alexandra Hinojosa was no ordinary student, and so it was worth opening old wounds and revisiting forgotten dreams.

Alexandra came to the Lowden Street house by herself one day in the early spring. She knocked. She was a slight girl of about twelve, carrying a violin case like so many others, with olive skin, long dark hair and deep brown eyes that darted away between glances. Was this a place of lessons? she asked. It was a question no one had asked of Sonia before. Yes, of course, Sonia answered, impatient, because Alexandra had disturbed her as she was paying bills, an activity that Sonia hated. I would like to learn, Alexandra said. Who is this child? Sonia wondered, and she realized she must have appeared stern or even angry—but then no one had ever come to her door and asked for lessons in person. The mothers of prospective students usually called her to schedule a first lesson. Their children were almost always Jewish or Italian, Chinese, or Korean. The women who called were the wives of doctors and lawyers, who were often doctors and lawyers themselves. They were second and third generation people, people who acted as if they had been in America forever, who spoke unaccented English and treated Sonia as if she were selling carpet or insurance, as if she had called *them* and not the other way around. As if she were not to be trusted. As if she were a servant or a tradeswoman. And not who she really was after all.

She brought the girl into her house and helped her off with her coat. Alexandra's instrument was a disaster, but then no child's violin is any good. The instrument had been in a closet. It looked as though no one had touched it in forty years. So Sonia took out her second instrument and handed it to the girl. How did you find me? Sonia said, expecting to hear about a referral from the small city symphony orchestra where Sonia was a first violin or about a school friend who was Sonia's student. I walk this way home, Alexandra said. I see other kids coming out of cars. With violins.

In fact, there *was* a school a few blocks away, and there was also a neighborhood of recent immigrants and boarded up houses about a quarter mile away in a different direction, down a hill and across a commercial street. A neighborhood of abandoned cars, broken pavement, and foreign grocery stores with garish flashing lights in their windows. Perhaps Alexandra had found her way to Sonia's house completely on her own. Perhaps.

At least there were no bad habits to break. Alexandra had never even held a violin. Sonia wondered if Alexandra had ever heard any of the music before. But she showed Alexandra, one small step at a time as she tried to remember how to talk about a process that, for Sonia, was as natural as breathing. Tighten and rosin the bow. The strange and uncomfortable placement of the left hand, so the fingers can move about the strings. How the instrument is placed against the neck, under the chin. Sonia remembered herself struggling to hold an instrument that was too large for her, in a cold room, in a four-story walk-up flat. On the street below, the trams ran every few minutes. When you looked out you saw leafless trees, tram wires, trams and many people in the street, walking in the cold, weak light of the northern winter. I want you to do nothing but hold the instrument for an hour a day until we meet again next week, Sonia said, doubting that she'd ever see the girl again. Let me show you one more time.

And then Sonia stood, feet apart, and lifted the instrument to her. She stayed perfectly still like that for a long moment, with no part of her moving at all, so Alexandra could see how it was done. Then Sonia drew the bow across a single string, a single long D.

Sonia played this single note, a note shaking with depth and overtones, a note that made every object in the room resonate, so that every picture-frame and teacup, bowl, and lamp shade trembled slightly with their own inner music. I'll never see the girl again, Sonia thought, as Alexandra's wide eyes turned from Sonia to the violin itself.

When Alexandra put her own instrument back in its case with hands that were still too small to play, her movements were careful and quick, as if she were handling an ancient family bible, an object of reverence. She doesn't know you pay for lessons, Sonia realized, as she gave the girl a time for the next week. Then Sonia stood at the storm door and watched the girl walk down the walk to the street. It's only a few minutes, Sonia told herself. These people are new in the country. They have different music. Different traditions. Sweet child, but clueless. She can't do much harm with that instrument, but it will frustrate her. She won't be back.

It is strange to remember and strange to live again in the memories that come back without effort when you least expect them.

Her own beginning was completely different. Sonia had

emerged in a world of buildings, of trams and books—and of music. She remembered her parents taking turns reading stories to her at night, and she remembered Mozart, Haydn, and Beethoven along with the stories. Although now she could remember the melody and the phrasing of the music more clearly than she could recall the stories themselves. Peter and Katrinka. Ice skates. Racing on the ice. Little boys falling through the ice. Mozart Concerto #4. Handel Concerto Grosso Opus 3 Number 4 in F. The Last Quartets. The radio and their record player which Sonia's father valued more than anything else, the records smuggled in from Moscow and Tel Aviv.

She was four. Her father didn't play well. The instrument came from a pawnshop. He bought it early one spring when there was no food in the stores to spend money on. In the days before he lost his position at the university and began to work as a clerk in a dry cleaner's, before he left for America. The seam between the back and side was open and the fingerboard had come off. Sonia's mother was angry when he first brought it home. Wasteful, she said, just fantasy. We need bread and meat. But Sonia's father, who could fix anything, found a friend with hide glue. He and his friend put the instrument back together and then there it was, restrung, ready to play and almost as big as Sonia herself.

One night, when Sonia's parents' friends had gathered and two of their friends were playing, Sonia lifted the violin. Four. She was only four years old and it was way past her bedtime. She stood up on a chair and said, I will play for you now a concert. Her parents and their friends laughed and applauded. Her father helped her hold the instrument for the first time. Sonia was so small that her left hand could barely reach the top of the violin's sound box so her father stood behind her and held the fingerboard. Even then the bow was too heavy for her small hand, so her father reached around and held her hand in his as he placed her hand and the bow on the strings. But it was Sonia who drew the bow. Her father, in his wisdom, angled the bow just right. Sonia could still feel the heat from her father's warm chest as a note that was bigger than the whole house filled the room and spread through her body, sweet and clear and long.

The girl came back ten minutes past the appointed time. The narcissus was up against the white fence but had not finished blooming. The sand on the streets that had been used to create traction when there was ice everywhere had not yet been swept away by rains and by street sweepers. Alexandra was wearing a red spring coat that was too long and too thin for the coolness of the day. Sonia helped her off with her coat and went to the kitchen to turn on the electric kettle so she could make Alexandra a cup of tea. When she came back to the parlor, Alexandra had the instrument out of the case and was holding the violin exactly as Sonia had shown her to hold it. She was standing in the window, so the slanted warm yellow light of later afternoon bathed her face and upper body.

When Sonia came into the room, Alexandra drew the bow over the G string. The note was long and clean. Then the girl up-bowed, a stirring and clear A. Sonia inhaled with the up-bowing and that breath, which was a breath of pure pleasure, now suffused her body, so she stood taller and fuller than she had a few moments before. I did not tell you to play, Sonia said. I told you to just hold the instrument, nothing more. An hour a day. I did not give permission for the playing of notes. The little girl lowered the instrument, her face deflated, and Sonia hoped that the girl was not able to see any of the pleasure that Sonia felt in her face or the joy she felt inside herself. They do not know punctuality or how to follow directions, Sonia thought. She will not be back.

Alexandra came the next week at the appointed time. It was raining hard that day, and the thin red coat was soaked through.

Alexandra's plain white blouse was grey on the shoulders, front and back now, glistening wet and cold to the touch. I'm getting you something to wear, Sonia said, and she brought a thick wool sweater from her bedroom. Change into this, Sonia said, the bathroom is down the hall, the second door on the left.

The girl was ludicrously thin, lost in that sweater, Sonia thought, as she put Alexandra's blouse into the dryer. But this time the girl stood and played all the open notes. Her blouse had dried by the time their session was over.

It wasn't perfect. It never is. One day, Alexandra came early enough to see the previous student, a blond boy of twelve with a future as a scientist or a soccer player, finish his lesson. She saw the boy's mother get out her checkbook, scribble on it, tear off a check and hand the check to Sonia before they walked out. Sonia could sense Alexandra brooding about what she had seen. Alexandra was tense and distracted all during the lesson. Sonia waited for Alexandra to ask about what lessons cost, but the child didn't seem to have the words she needed. This girl needs to learn about how the world works, Sonia thought, although Sonia did not want either to cause the girl embarrassment or to let the girl off the hook.

In the summer, Alexandra missed a lesson, confirming what Sonia already knew. She's had it. She's done. No discipline. They don't know anything about this music. Why should she care? Her people listen to salsa and country music or top forty hits on the radio, and that is enough for them. She had wasted time giving away free lessons to a girl who could not possibly benefit from the attention. Just more wasted time in a life wasted on pursuits that went nowhere.

But the next week, Alexandra appeared at the appointed time. No words about the missed lesson passed between them. I am going to the Cape for two weeks, Sonia said at the end of the lesson. Here is your assignment, week by week, so I will see you in not one, not two, but three Tuesdays from now, at the usual time. I expect you to be on time. If you must ever miss a lesson again, you must call me the day before. I require twenty-four hour notice.

And then something occurred to Sonia. She went into the kitchen where she kept her business cards and brought back a card and a pencil. This is my name, Sonia said. And this is my telephone number, she said, as she circled her number on the card. They had been working together for four months, and Sonia realized that Alexandra didn't know the first thing about her, not even her name, and Sonia didn't know the first thing about Alexandra. Then Sonia went back to the kitchen and found an index card. Write your name, address, and telephone number here, Sonia said. That way if I ever have to cancel, I can call you the day before as well.

That card, written in pencil, in block letters that were not precisely formed, would live ever-after on the corkboard next to the telephone in Sonia's hall. Next to the cards of the plumber, the electrician, the taxicab company, the police and fire departments and the number of rescue, on the corkboard where Sonia's eye's rested whenever she answered the telephone. The must-have information needed to maitain a life.

In two years' time, Alexandra became brilliant, the student all teachers wish for, the student who would surpass her. Alexandra was not a great violinist by any means. Not yet. But she was a great student. She learned quickly and somehow in her fingers there appeared emotion, the one aspect of musicianship that Sonia did not know how to teach. This girl, who barely spoke and whose command of English wasn't certain, understood in some part of her what the music meant, and that understanding came out through her fingers and in her phrasing. Her technique was good, yes, and she rapidly developed the strength and dexterity to play, strength and dexterity that comes only from practicing three, four, even six hours a day. But this girl had something more. She had the music hidden in her soul, and it sprang from her as if it were caged and struggling to be released from this thin, simple, lost body.

Sonia was a good teacher, but soon Alexandra would need a great teacher. Someone who could frighten her and drive her, but also a teacher quietly connected to great performers and great orchestras. A teacher quietly sought out by the world's great ones, who come from far away to take a private lesson, looking to find a new tone or polish a texture so they can go from confident and musical to great and stirring; from polite applause to twenty minutes of a standing ovation. She would have to go to Boston or New York to live, and she would have to give her whole life to the music, to do what Sonia had been unable to do, and to realize what Sonia had been unable to realize.

Sonia's first teacher had made those connections for Sonia when she herself was twelve, just a girl living in Buda. She had been thin herself, thin and quite pale, just old enough to understand the paleness of her parents and know the meaning of the numbers on their arms, and just aware enough to know their anxieties and sleeplessness, which had become her sleeplessness and her anxieties. She was old enough to remember the red stars, the red flags, and the huge public statues, and also old enough to remember when the trams ran every five minutes and were free. Old enough to remember always knowing that there were many places and many schools where she could not go because of who she was, but too young to remember the Russian tanks when they rolled through the streets in 1956. There was always music in their flat, even when there was little joy.

Sonia's first teacher brought her to Simhousen when she was

twelve. The great man looked through her as she took her instrument out of the case. Is this one strong enough? she sensed he was asking himself as she lifted her instrument. He was thinking, will she stand up to what I am going to demand that she does, or will she crack? On top of everything else. In spite of it. In those years no one spoke of what they had lived through because all of them had lived through it together, and words about it conveyed nothing, compared to what it meant to have survived.

But Simhousen was shocked when Sonia played. She was so thin. Simhousen was accustomed to precision from students brought to him to audition. He knew virtuosity. But Sonia surprised him. The story of what they had experienced came through her even though she had not experienced any of it herself. The pain. The fear. The loneliness. The cold and the starvation and the exhaustion. The loss. The endless losses. Their survival, yes, the survival, but only as a fragment of what had been before. A whole world, entirely lost. It was all there in her playing. Miraculous. Simhousen stood up while she played, and then he paced. Five years of work, endless work, he said. And then perhaps. Only perhaps. I am not certain she will last.

Now the great teacher, the great man, was a woman, Vivienne Liung. She was ten years younger than Sonia and was better known as a teacher than she was as a performer. She had studied with the great teachers who taught Sonia's generation, she had performed all over the world, she had won the major competitions and then she had withdrawn from performing to teach. She had also studied with Simhousen, though in the last years of the great man's life.

Vivienne was coming to Providence in November for thirty-six hours as a guest soloist with the orchestra. The orchestra would rehearse on its own for six weeks before the performance and then would rehearse once with Vivienne the night before the concert. Vivienne would give a masterclass in the early afternoon on the day of the concert. Then a radio interview. Then a stop at Brown to be on a panel. Then a performance, and then off to New York by train in the morning.

Sonia, who had been first violin in the Rhode Island Philharmonic for 30 years, heard in May that Vivienne was coming. The pieces were announced, the scores distributed, and the orchestra would begin rehearsals for those pieces in early October. It was a hobby, playing in that orchestra. A little orchestra in a little provincial town. Just to keep her hand in, and to attract students. Teaching kept Sonia alive now.

There was an intermediary in London, a friend with whom Sonia had played with in Budapest before she emigrated. Emails went back and forth. I have a promising student Vivienne should hear. The friend in London had to remind Vivienne who Sonia was, who she studied with, who she had been and who she could have become.

Vivienne finally responded. There are a few minutes in the late afternoon. Have her come to my hotel. Have her prepare three difficult pieces. She should expect me to grill her. To push her. To try to break her. There is some of the old man in me, Vivienne wrote, once she understood Sonia's lineage.

By this time, the girl had become more presentable, but there was still a part of Alexandra that Sonia didn't know. Many parts. Alexandra had achieved technical mastery of all the pieces Sonia rehearsed with her. She stood correctly. She breathed correctly. Her tone was perfect and her phrasing was immaculate, so good that Sonia didn't understand how she had come by it. As her technique improved, Alexandra had learned to look the part of a performer. Sonia brought her to hear the orchestra when they played, to rehearsals and to performances, picking her up in front of her house in that neighborhood that was both close by and very far away, and dropping her there after the performance, before Sonia joined the others for coffee or vodka and to decompress.

Alexandra took a black skirt Sonia gave her, added a white blouse, and learned to look perfectly respectable. Her long dark brown hair was now brushed back and hung almost to her waist, reflecting the order and luster of hundreds of brush strokes. Her ochre skin added depth to the whiteness of her blouse. Her almost black eyes, opaque and subterranean at the same time, made her appear close and mysterious at once.

But Sonia didn't know how Alexandra lived. Sonia had never been in Alexandra's house, which was on an ignored street that few people knew. It was a pale green and grey-white triple-decker with almost no yard and a broken-up cement driveway that had a grape arbor in front of it made from old iron pipes. The tiny porch with three rotting steps and no handrail led to two doors. Next to each door was a line of doorbells and nameplates, but most of the name cards were scratched out, written over or just blank. Alexandra was almost always on the porch, outside, waiting when Sonia came for her. When Sonia let her off at home after a concert, she stayed in front of the house, the car running and the lights on until Alexandra had the key in the lock and the door open, because there was no working porch-light, and because, well, just to be safe.

And Sonia didn't know Alexandra's people. No mother had ever brought Alexandra for a lesson or picked her up after the lesson was over. Alexandra answered the door herself whenever Sonia rang it. No one else—no sister, father, uncle, or a grandmother—ever came to the door to say Alexandra will be down in a moment, why don't you come in.

The concert started at eight. Come to my hotel at 5:45 and I'll listen to your student, Vivienne had written. The hotel is next to the Vets. I'll listen, and then we can walk to the concert hall together.

I'll come and get you at five, Sonia told Alexandra. Be ready, Sonia said. Don't be late. Dress appropriately. Everything depends on this day.

As she drove to Alexandra's house on the day of the audition, Sonia remembered how she thought her life would be after Simhousen, after the great man blessed her, and how different her life was from those dreams. She thought, I will practice all the time. I will perform in Budapest but also in Prague, Vienna, Berlin, Frankfurt, Moscow, Venice, and Tel Aviv. And then in London, Boston and New York. I will have a large airy flat overlooking the Danube with its own practice room, and I will marry a conductor or a great cellist. We will have a country house. Before long I will teach master classes of my own and learn to frighten the best students, so we find and train the great ones, frightening off those without an inner being made of steel, and leaving the others to give lessons or play in the orchestras of small cities or to do something else entirely, to become computer programmers or dermatologists or engineers.

Sonia practiced all the time. She won the competitions that must be won. She performed with the orchestras and got the kind of reviews soloists dream of. One step led to another, which was certain to lead to a third. First a chair in the orchestra. Then a solo career.

But when Sonia was ready to step up, all the chairs in the orchestra were full. None of the violinists were retiring. The generation who Sonia should have replaced had been killed off or had fled twenty years before. Those who filled their seats, whose playing was perhaps not at the level of the pre-war years, were in those seats nonetheless and didn't plan on leaving for another twenty years. Prague or Moscow, perhaps. But nothing at all in Budapest.

Then there was political turmoil and with turmoil came years of shortages before the wall came down, and then came a few years of chaos and more shortages.

In those years of turmoil, the established pathways to a secure place had fallen apart. You couldn't simply go from Budapest to

Moscow anymore and in Moscow earn the respect needed to travel internationally. Instead, you had to emigrate and start all over in London, New York, or Tel Aviv.

Then suddenly it became possible to travel and even to emigrate.

Sonia met a chemist after one of her performances, a chemist who knew the music. When Leonid courted her, he promised London and New York. But after they married, and there was Sasha and Karl, they came to Rhode Island, not New York, for a university position. With the university position came the undergraduates and the graduate students, too many of whom were young women, and then, in a flash, Sonia's imagined life was gone.

Sonia parked outside Alexandra's house. There were no lights on inside the house, but there was still daylight. Alexandra was not waiting on the porch. Sonia honked her horn. It was five of five. There was still time.

Vivienne and Sonia walked together from the hotel to the concert hall.

We know that only a very few will progress. The process of finding and training those few is long and difficult. The life itself has many limitations. Many doors have to be closed along the way. The discipline is withering. Some doors can never be imagined. There is no shame in trying, in testing.

Vivienne and Sonia did not speak of these things, of course. They spoke only of Simhousen. They both remembered the strength of the great man's grip when he shook a person's hand and the power of his embrace when he hugged you after not seeing you for a long time. How when he held you, he seemed to be holding onto life itself.

Sonia, before and after her apology, could not think and she could not feel. Her ability to feel anything ended forever while she was standing on that porch, as she rang the bell and knocked on that door again and again at five-fifteen, until five-thirty. A short bearded man in a tee-shirt, wearing only green plaid undershorts, stumbled to the other door, barely awake, or barely sober or both, having been woken by Sonia's voice and her persistent hard rapping. No here, he said, when he saw her knocking on the other door. No home. And then he turned away, closed his door, and walked back up the stairs.

Even so, Vivienne treated her with respect. Sonia had studied with the old man. Vivienne knew now who Sonia once was. And who she could have been.

The concertmaster came on stage as the orchestra was warming up, each instrument making a note or two to test the precision of their tuning. Together they created a bright cacophony of hopes and expectations. The concertmaster stood, raised his bow, and the instruments quieted. He sat. The conductor came on the stage to applause, waved and then bowed. The conductor went to the microphone and said a few words about the program and each piece. Then he introduced Vivienne, who took the stage confidently, wearing a low-cut black silk dress and pearls. She stood in a spotlight, waiting for her cue.

Sonia sat stage left, in the row of first violins.

The conductor raised his baton.

Sonia drew her bow across the strings. The note Sonia played was sweet, long and clear. It came not from her instument but from inside Sonia herself, from her chest and pelvis, from her belly and her back, from her thighs and shoulders. Her body and soul wrapped itself around that note, perfecting its pitch and intonation as the note went free, tuned by every part of her.

Sonia hated Alexandra in that moment and loved her. She hated life and loved it.

The note joined itself to the timbre and tone of the orchestra's rising sound, which felt as if it was ascending to heaven itself. And then it disappeared.

FROM ALL MEN

When Arthur Rubinow, the shamesh, the haysedonda (the person who says 'Hey! Sit down there!') of the Meeting Street Shul, counted the people in his mind, he found only six. Eight for Mincha/Maariv today. Six for shacharit tomorrow. A minyan is ten. Ten men, once. Ten anyone, now. Ten Jews. He needed ten Jews to have a real service, ten people so that people saying Kaddish could mourn their dead correctly, with memory, honor and dignity, sing G-d's praises, read Torah and learn together.

They were a dwindling community, but they were a community nonetheless. Once upon a time, not so very long ago, the early morning minyan had been warm and vibrant. They davened in a chapel in the basement of the synagogue, a moldy place that faced east with walls made of dark wood that had thick stained-glass windows, which were pictures of trees with blue and green leaves, windows that let in, but mostly kept out, daylight. Thirty men, even in the middle of summer when families went to their beach houses for weeks at a time. Ten or fifteen women, who sat off to one side. There was never a wall or even a curtain between the men and the women. They were not a community that needed a wall. People just knew where to sit and everyone respected everyone else.

Before, most of the men had come from Europe, most from before and some after the war. They worked in or ran businesses: a candy factory owner, a furrier, a dry cleaner, a junk dealer whose children would call him a recycler of used building material after they got into real estate, a furniture store owner, a couple of sales clerks, a jeweler or two, a rug dealer, and the owner of the little department store in Central Falls whose father started as a peddler walking from place to place, carrying his wares on his back. The Hebrew teachers and the Jewish community people, the functionaries who ran the Federation and the JCC and HIAS and the Hebrew Free Loan fund, they came as well, but less often than you might think, because by and large they were American-born, and didn't feel the pain of history and the sadness of unrequited longing in their souls the way the generation who had been born in the shtetl or in Warsaw or Budapest or Bucharest or Prague did.

Their children, the second generation, the doctors and lawyers and engineers, were different. Some came as children and continued to come, in smaller and smaller numbers, after they grew up, but most didn't come at all. That generation didn't really know how to daven even though they could read the words. They used Sephardic pronunciation and sometimes even Sephardic trope— even though their families were from Eastern Europe—because that was the way Hebrew was spoken now, in what Arthur Rubinow always called the new state of Israel even though it was 60 years old, which he prayed for with his heart and soul but never entirely believed could survive. The second generation came because their fathers came, out of respect and a little fear, the ones who were given to respect and fear though many of that generation and most of the generation which came after them ran wild in the streets.

That older generation, the generation of immigrants, they really knew. They knew Torah, they knew Talmud, they knew how to daven, to pray with their whole souls, and they had sachel, wisdom. They listened before speaking and they turned a problem or idea over in their minds, thinking out all the ramifications before answering a question or stating their beliefs. More often than not, they answered a question with a question. Who is a fool? Solomon ibn Gabirol asks. Then answers: He who knows not and knows not he knows not. Who is wise? the Pirkei Avot asks? And answers: he who learns from all men.

When the minyan was at its height, the chapel would be full twice a day. Sometimes the late comers, the people who lived in the suburbs and arrived a few minutes late or the men who stayed at business a little too long in the late afternoon, they would have to stand in the back. The late comers had to use cast-off siddurim, the old prayer books which had different page numbers and worn covers.

Each of the regulars had a seat, of course, and every man knew who would lead which part of the service at which time and on what day. On Mondays and Thursdays, when they read Torah, everyone knew who would get the first Aliyah and everyone knew that the last two, before and after the misheberach, the blessing for the sick, were reserved for guests or newcomers so that even the young men, who often came trailed by a son or a boy and girl of four and six, had a job to do and a place in the community and felt included and respected. Each man shook the hand of every other man after their part or after an aliyah, so by the time the davening was finished, every man had shaken the hand of every other man in the community ten or twenty times. Yes, just the men. That was normal. Part of daily life, something no one even noticed or questioned but which happened every single day of the year nonetheless.

But then the generation from Europe began to die out. The

doctors and lawyers and accountants came, but only once or twice a week, or only on shabbos, or only mornings or only evenings and gradually not at all. The minyan thinned. There was a moment in the late seventies and eighties when the Russians arrived and it looked like the minyan might grow again. But the Russians didn't last. Their old men knew how to read but they didn't know Torah and Talmud, they didn't daven with their souls the way the old men born in Poland, Galicia, Romania and Lithuania did, and the Russian men didn't mix much with the rest of the minyan. The old Russian men died off quickly, and their second generation didn't come at all.

The minyan felt the loss of each man, of each person, the loss of the men who knew and their wives who came with them and sat off to the side. Each loss left a gap, a hole that could be felt and even seen, a lost tooth, because everyone in the minyan knew the voice of every other person, knew the way they would sing a certain part. What had been a robust and guttural chorus when the minyan sang or spoke the shema or the borachu or words or lines of the kaddish together became a few voices, singing alone together, the women's voices clearly heard now, and sweet, because most of the few women could at least carry a tune.

Sometimes only fifteen or twenty men came. Then only twelve or thirteen. Many seats went unfilled. The chapel was renovated and moved from the basement to the top of a flight of stairs, facing south, not east, so the sun streamed through the windows at sunset in winter, and the old dark wooden benches were replaced by blond wood chairs with nice upholstery.

They coped. First the shamash and the gabbai were replaced by men who were American born. Then they started counting women to make the minyan, as the need for ten men became the need for ten people. Then women had aliyahs and then women read from the Torah and then a woman became the gabbai. Who knew?

But despite all the change, the minyan shrank. Some days they waited fifteen or twenty minutes for a minyan. Some days thirty minutes. Some days an hour. Some days Arthur Rubinow called his friend Morty to come over to make ten. Some days he asked his wife Diane. They thought about and discussed opening the ark and counting the Holy Presence to help them get to ten people, as they did in some of the tiny communities in Galicia and Georgia, but then their Rabbi ruled against such a practice. There were enough Jews in the community to make a minyan. So the responsibility was to find more people to come. Was minyan attendance also the responsibility of the Holy One, Blessed be He? No! It was the responsibility of the community! But then the Rabbi himself didn't come any more, so what sense did any of it make?

Some days they didn't get ten people at all, and so mourners couldn't say Kaddish, they couldn't read Torah, and they couldn't recite the Shmoneh Esrei out loud or say the Kedusha at all.

There was a new minyan of hippies who met in the chapel on Shabbos after the early morning minyan was over, and the two groups met on the stairs or coming through the doors. The men had long hair and the women had tattoos and piercings, like Canaanite harlots or the Moabite ritual prostitutes described in Bereshit. They drummed and played guitars. Young people. But at least they came to shul.

Now everything was different. Women rabbis. Cantors who were converts. Gay men and lesbians and people who went from one gender to the other and back. There were people of color in that minyan. Chinese people and people from India and Africa, people whose skin was as black as charcoal. The world had changed. The people of the early morning minyan barely recognized the new world they were in.

One shabbos in early summer, when some of the regulars were

at the beach, when the sun was very strong even though it was early, only five people were sitting in the seats and only eight all together were coming. Two women. Three men. Five. Better than nothing. Still, Arthur Rubinow announced the page, and David Weinstein, a retired dentist, began the preliminary prayers. Everyone understood that Kaddish D'Rabbanan would be left out. People would trickle in, and some of those parts could be added back at the end of the service, once they got to ten. If they got to ten. If a miracle happened.

But Arthur Rubinow had already counted in his mind, and he knew a minyan was impossible. Diane Berkovits was at the beach. The Golds were visiting their son and new daughter-in-law in Bethesda. The Aroniwitzes were in the Berkshires. Arthur Kaplan just had foot surgery and couldn't walk yet. Arthur Rubinow had made his phone calls the evening before and he knew what he knew. Eight. With luck they might get eight. But no more. The world was full of Jews but no more than eight Jews in the whole city were available to pray together, read Torah and sing G-d's praises that day in late June.

The door lock buzzed. There were footsteps on the stairs. Penelope Yellin came in and took her usual seat, so now they were six. They did not say Borachu but they read the Shema out loud together. You can say the Shema alone so you can certainly say it with only six.

Arthur Rubinow closed his eyes and went out into the hallway where he could use his cellphone without being seen. Pikuach nefesh. It is permissible to break all rules in order to preserve life. Wasn't a minyan life itself? He texted Morty and Diane. Diane texted back. She was getting out of bed and would drive over. That would make seven. Jeffery Sussman, their Gabbai, would arrive right at 8:17 as he did every shabbos, just in time for the Torah reading. He was a lawyer and acted like the rules that applied to everyone else didn't apply to him. But he came every week, and that was enough for them. They might get to eight. But no more. Ten was impossible, at least this week. They would cope, they would go on living, and, G-d willing, they would have a minyan again shabbos the following week when people returned from their travels.

But a little part of Arthur Rubinow felt shame nonetheless. They were a community, and as a community they had failed to keep this small promise to themselves. He was a man, and he had failed to find ten people, in a world that was full of people, in a world that had once been full of men who wanted only to stand together, to sing G-d's praises, to remember, to give to charity, to do good deeds, and to carry on. Now there was almost nothing left. He had been delaying the inevitable and was unable to admit the truth. There just weren't enough people for a minyan anymore. He lived in a lost world.

They were ready to read the first Amidah. Waiting for more people wasn't going to change anything. The Amidah would have to be said silently, without the Kiddusha. Arthur Rubinow stood to announce the page.

But when Arthur Rubinow opened his mouth, a siren came out instead of words. An earsplitting, brilliantly painful, too-loud-to-think siren. WHHOP WHHOP WHHOP WHHOP. Who makes noises like this on shabbos? For a moment, Arthur Rubinow wondered if he was having a stroke and perhaps the siren was only in his brain. But the other people looked around, put down their siddurim, their prayer books, took off their tallesim, folded them, put them on their seats, and marched toward the doors. The siren was a fire alarm, and it was LOUD.

Arthur Rubinow followed the little group out the door, climbed down the stairs, and left the building.

Three fire trucks pulled up in front of the shul, their red and white lights bathing the streets. Two police cars arrived, adding blue and white lights to the red and white lights washing the buildings and the cars. The street smelled of diesel exhaust, though there was still a hint of the sweet green taste of late spring because of all the flowers and trees that were in bloom in the plantings and from the trees planted next to the street.

Teams of firefighters went into the building. The six people from the minyan clustered on the sidewalk in front of the stoop. The men still all wore kippas and the women wore white lace doilies pinned to their hair, but the little knot of people standing together looked somehow out of place, six Jews in nice clothing standing together on a bright June morning as firemen with red fire hats and yellow rubber fireman's boots stood in front of their trucks, trotted back and forth to the shul, or prowled inside the synagogue.

"I didn't smell smoke," Pauline Yellin said.

"Was my davening that bad that it set off the fire alarm?" David Weinstein asked.

Diane walked down the sidewalk and joined them. Jeffery Sussman arrived. Now they were eight. Eight Jews on a sidewalk. Too few and with no place to go.

The firemen walked in and out. A team of three, carrying an oxygen tank, came out of the building. Better they are coming out than rushing in with hoses, Arthur Rubinow thought. In a real fire we would need to go in ourselves to rescue and protect the Torahs. Six Torahs in the chapel alone. Many more in the main sanctuary and the vault.

More firemen came out.

The fire trucks turned off their flashing lights. Then the police cars drove away.

False alarm, Arthur Rubinow thought. We'll go in soon and finish. Only eight of us. No Torah reading. We'll finish fast.

"How long do we wait?" David Weinstein said.

Arthur Rubinow approached a group of firefighters who stood in front of the first truck, killing time. Two smoked cigarettes.

"Gentlemen, are we free to return to the building?' he said. "Fire, or false alarm?"

"No false alarms, only tests of systems integrity," one of the firefighters said. His hat was under his arm. He had a ruddy complexion, a thinning hairline, and a bushy moustache.

"No fire. If there was a fire we wouldn't be standing here, blowing smoke," said a second firefighter, who was tall, dark-skinned and powerfully built.

"Ya gotta wait for the Fire Marshall to sing," said a young one, who was fair and pale, slight but with big shoulders and blue and green tattoos that flowed over his arms and neck, who had close cropped red hair and green eyes. "They check carefully. I think he's almost done. Hey, Shabbat Shalom, Mr. Rubinow, it's Neil Green."

Arthur Rubinow took half a step backward. Neil Green was a little boy, a mischief maker, a pipsqueak, who came to shul only once in a blue moon, when his divorced father, an animator for a film studio, was in town and came to say Kaddish. The mother was a teacher and was Portuguese. She converted when the kid was born, but lost interest as soon as the father moved out. Neil Green. He was always a kid Arthur Rubinow gave candy to when he came, so his memories of Torah would always be sweet. Who knew?

"No hurry," Arthur Rubinow said. "We're only eight. We'll be done in five minutes."

Two men in orange hats came out of a side door. They were older guys, in their forties or early fifties, ruddy faced and beefy.

"All clear," one of them said. "You can go back now."

We'll have to hurry, Arthur Rubinow thought. We started twenty minutes late. We davened for ten or fifteen minutes before the fire alarm and have been twenty or thirty minutes outside. The hippies with their drumming will be here before long. Start on Page 115. It shouldn't take us long.

The others were starting to go inside.

A young man wearing a kippah and carrying a tallis bag walked toward the shul. Or perhaps it was not a young man. The person walking had long hair that was held in place by a hairband, and glasses, and wore a white shirt and trousers. One of the hippies coming to drum, a little early.

"Shabbat Shalom," the person said, and held the door for Arthur Rubinow.

"Shabbat Shalom," Arthur Rubinow replied. "Can you daven with us? We don't have a minyan yet. We'll be done in ten minutes."

"Of course," the person said.

They walked up the stairs together, both of them. One more person. A little closer to a minyan, and perhaps a little closer to G-d.

Then the buzzer went off. Someone was at the locked door. It was one of the firemen. Neil Green. Arthur Rubinow went down the stairs to let him in.

"I can stay until we get another call," Neil Green said. "The boys on the truck'll wait. Cap'n's good with it."

Arthur Rubinow and Neil Green, this pipsqueak, now a man, also walked up the stairs together, also both of them.

They had ten. Ten including two people neither Arthur Rubinow nor any of the other regulars even knew existed. They were a community, however thrown together by accident, however worn out, accidental and ragtag, and together they could daven together, remember the past, mourn the dead, and learn.

The world had changed under their feet while the people of

the early morning minyan weren't looking. Neither better nor worse. Just different.

What is holy? G-d is holy. Kindness is holy. Justice is holy.

Who is wise? He, and now she, and now they, who learn from all men. And women. And everything and everyone else in between.

THE BLIND EMPEROR

Nothing is the way it used to be.

Once upon a time, Federal Hill was for Italians. The Episcopalians and the Quakers lived on College Hill. The Jews lived in South Providence and Smith Hill. Mount Hope was Black. Fox Point was Portuguese and Cape Verdean, although to tell the truth, we thought the Cape Verdeans were Blacks who didn't get the part about Mount Hope. The French Canadians lived in Woonsocket, Central Falls and Pawtucket. The Polish lived in Central Falls. The Greeks lived in Cranston. The Irish lived everywhere else, and there were no Dominicans, Puerto Ricans, Columbians, Guatemalans, Mexicans, Salvadorians, Nigerians, Liberians, Ghanaians, Sierra Leoneans, Hmong, Cambodians, Nepalese or Malians—nothing like that. Life was simpler then. You knew who was who and what was what. A man was a man. A woman was a woman. A kid was a kid. One plus one still equaled two. No new math. No finessing. You knew who you were and what you were and what to expect. Even when it sucked. Which it did sometimes, for some people. And for some people way more than others. But most of us, we took what we were given, loved who we loved, hated who we hated, and just sucked it up when shit happened. Which it did. Often. In the days before you could write and say curse words in public, before women even knew what they had was called a vagina and before men knew that they were supposed to think and feel, to be anything other than brutes.

Abe Klein inherited the place. It was the family business, a business that came to Abe when his father, the reigning Blind Emperor, had a stroke at 83. Abe never imagined he'd be back in Providence or ever have anything to do with the Blind Emperor again, but here he was.

The Blind Emperor was the inspiration and invention of Abe's great-grandmother Sophie, a short, squat, swarthy Yiddish-speaking woman from Russia–Poland, who came steerage to the US with two infants in 1902. Sophie had followed her husband of five years from Poland to Danzig, to Ellis Island, to the Lower East Side, and then to Providence, where she found that her husband was living on Orms Street with a new wife and two new babies on the third floor of a triple-decker in a two-room cold-water flat.

So Abe's great-grandmother Sophie found her own cold-water flat. She took in piece-work jewelry and washing to survive, working for women who themselves had to work twelve or fourteen hours a day in retail or making jewelry or in one of Rhode Island's hundreds of mills, mills that made worsted wool, locomotives, screws, underwear, or wire.

Before long the husband of some of the women Sophie washed for bought houses. Some of those houses had venetian blinds. Those blinds needed to be cleaned once or twice a year. Soon those women's husbands started to take down the venetian blinds in the spring and fall, carry them over to Sophie's house, and Sophie cleaned them. And thus a business was born.

The Blind Emperor. Sophie might have been short and squat. She might have worn dark European clothing in all the pictures Abe had of her. She might have had glasses with bottle-thick lenses, but she also had a certain grandiose style—she wanted all her family and friends to know how successful she was in America, and how important she and her family had become, despite her disgrace, despite the abandonment by her husband. So it wasn't the Blind Store. Or Venetian Blind Shop. Or even Window Coverings International. No. It was The Blind Emperor. A name that made it clear Sophie was a woman to be reckoned with, and that Sophie was in control.

Abe never knew his great-grandmother, of course. She died at fifty-six of stomach cancer, worn down by a life of toil, of stress and physical labor, ten years before Abe was born.

Sophie's son, Abe's grandfather Sol, worked in the Blind Emperor his whole life as well. Abe's father Manny went to Brown and almost escaped. He was a socialist, and for a brief period, a member of the Communist Party. His degree was in European History with a concentration in the revolutions of 1848. He went to law school in 1938. Then the Second World War broke out. Abe's father enlisted and was sent to the Pacific. When the war ended, Abe's grandfather couldn't find help in the shop and so Abe's father came home and worked in the store just to tide his father over. But one day led to the next and Abe's father stayed. He became the Blind Emperor himself, the man to come to for blinds, on the East side of Providence, in Barrington and East Greenwich and even as far away as Newport and Fall River and the South Shore. The emperor of all the blinds he could see.

Abe, on the other hand, was a different sort of human being.

He was an intellectual, and esthete, a child of the sixties, and he wanted no part of the family business. He learned to read at four and read everything he could get his hands on. He went to Classical High School but almost flunked out. He frustrated his teachers because they could tell he knew the answers to their questions, and often knew more about the material they were teaching than they did, but he couldn't be bothered to hand in the assignments, take tests, talk in class, or write papers. Then Abe spent five years in a VW minibus as an anti-war deadhead, traveling around the US, stoned out of his mind. Five lost years. No memory at all of what had happened, of where he'd been or what he'd done other than gauzy dreams and occasional flashbacks, all out of context.

And then suddenly, coherence. Abe awoke one day in the East Village as a clerk at the Strand bookstore, living on East 7th Street between Avenues C and D, shelving some books and taking others home to read. He read and he learned. One day he got to talking with a brilliant young woman in a tight black top about Walter Benjamin. She told him about the New School, which was just a few blocks away on 13th Street, and invited him to sit in on a course she was teaching. He learned that Hannah Arendt, Erich Fromm and Hans Jonas taught at the New School. Then he started taking their courses, and before he knew it, Abe had become an unreconstructed European intellectual of the Frankfurt School, with a PhD in Philosophy and an interest in Epistemology and Critical Theory, teaching at NYU and the New School. He smoked like a fiend, gesticulated with his hands when he spoke, marched with the Socialist Internationale whenever they marched, and spent his evenings in obscure bars like the Frog Pond and the Ukrainian National Home and Restaurant, discussing the fine points of the Hegelian roots of Marxist thought and the anarcho-syndicalist theory of science with colleagues and students from all over the country and the world.

Abe lived with a succession of women in those years, one more distracted and depressed than the next. Somehow, beautiful women were attracted to him, although Abe himself was nothing to look at—hunched over, bearded and bald, with bottle-thick glasses like his grandmother's, beady eyes and pasty skin, part intellectual, part stevedore and part Talmudist. Women were pulled in by Abe's complete absorption in the world of ideas. He never saw them, not for one second. The more beautiful the woman, the more she couldn't resist the temptation to be seen, to be noticed and to be known by Abe. But to Abe, the women in his life were a distraction from his real work, and he paid them no mind, even when one moved in for a few months and tried her best to make Abe look at her and see into her soul.

Except for one. Lily. Lily the Mexican poet in exile. They met one May in Tompkins Square Park, playing speed chess on the first warm day of spring, when the pigeons were everywhere, circling over the park. Lily was dark-haired and dark-complected, with brilliant eyes that were more black than brown. She was a fierce chess player. She beat Abe five games in a row, with each successive victory taking her less time so that Abe was on his knees, from the perspective of chess, inside an hour, as Lily quickly learned how his mind worked and used that knowledge to demolish his game.

Abe was mesmerized so he pursued Lily—the first time in his life Abe had put any effort at all into a relationship with a woman. He brought her flowers. He called her. He waited on the front stoop of her building on East Second Street until she came home at 4 AM, as the dawn was breaking over the East River. He took her out, once, on the Staten Island Ferry, to an Italian place on the Staten Island waterfront, and once, on the back of a motorcycle, to the Delaware Water Gap, to the river between New Jersey and Pennsylvania. He drove all the way to Mexico City when she went home to stay for two months in the winter, when she got tired of the cold.

Truth be told, Abe and Lily were more alike than different. They were both the great-grandchildren of immigrant Eastern European Jews. Both lived in a world distant from the world most people lived in, the world of ideas, abstractions, and unique vocabularies, and both believed the world we have is not the world they wanted to live in, that the world needed improvement, which they were somehow empowered to create.

But Abe, try as he might, failed to win Lily's heart. He spent so much time in his own head, and had so many distractions that, though he was given to grand gestures, he was never really present when he and Lily were together. What all those other women fell in love with when they fell in love with Abe was Abe's absence. What Lily wanted was his presence. Or perhaps a different kind of presence all together, a man who would make her knees shake whenever he walked into a room. And Abe was just not that kind of man.

One day, when he was out marching down Fifth Avenue protesting one invasion or another, Lily moved her things out of Abe's apartment and he never saw her again. He wondered for a bit when she wasn't home when he got home. It took two days for him to figure out that she had gone.

The sixties became the seventies; the seventies became the eighties, and then the nineties and then Y2K. The city Abe knew transformed itself from a place of the heart and the mind to a place of steel and money, where graffiti was replaced by skyscrapers, where there were flowers in all the flowerbeds and the parks were clean and safe, instead of scruffy and real. US colonialism didn't disappear. It just faded away, replaced by a new kind of capitalism and a new kind of materialism. The global economy. Money and work, not ideas, justice, beauty, family, friends, and love. Technology driving the human experience, just like Marx said it would. No class consciousness. Not even any classes, not really. Just consumers. No life of the mind.

Then, out of this sad coherence, chaos again. Abe's father had a stroke. Someone needed to run the store until they could wind things down and sell the building. No one cleans venetian blinds anymore. Yes, they had moved into window fashions. Yes, they had every size and color of mini-blinds imaginable—custom awnings, drapery, canopies, motorized window coverings, quilted curtains to keep in the heat, tinted applications that let in only certain wavelengths of sunlight—you name it, and the Blind Emperor had it or could get it overnight. Abe's father had done a bang-up job, keeping the Blind Emperor up to speed in the market, becoming the Blind Emperor in fact.

Abe would run the place for a week, not a month. Until Abe and his sister could get Abe's parents situated. But not one day more than that. Only until they could figure out how much function Abe's father had lost and how much might come back.

A week turned into a month. A month turned into a year. One year turned into ten.

To his surprise, Abe found he liked the work. He liked the challenge of keeping track of ten different things at once. He liked running numbers in his head. Abe worked in the store in high school, and knew how to run the business, almost instinctively, as though venetian blinds were in his genome. He knew how to check inventory and order stock. How to keep your eye on your employees, because if you turn your back for one second even the good ones will steal from you. How to do payroll and make bank deposits, make sure payroll taxes are paid and the income tax filings are done on time.

Abe loved his employees and loved hearing about their lives, which were sometimes chaotic but more often lives of hard work, family love and human decency. There were even some customers he liked, even though most were made-up young women from the suburbs who drove him crazy. Their materialism was part of the problem. But their thousands of questions and constant negotiation—for a better price, a better color, about the time of day of delivery and so forth, made Abe despair for the human condition, the same old despair that he used to think about abstractly when he read the newspaper in the morning, only now it was a despair that was present close-up and personal every single day. Reified. That was the word that Kant or Heidegger or even Habermas would have used. Abe's world was real now. In a way he never planned for or anticipated.

One day at noon, when Abe was in the store by himself, a young woman came into the store alone. She had tan skin, deep brown eyes that were more black than brown, and long pink and blue hair that had once been almost black. She was much younger than most of the women who came into the store. Than all of the women who came into the store. Probably ever.

She came right to the counter. Pierced lips, nose, cheek, and eyebrow. Tattoos everywhere. Maybe she was after a handout. Lots of drug-addicted people on the street now. The imminent collapse of late phase capitalism. Better she asks than steals, at least from me, Abe thought. She could be anyone or anything. But was more likely trouble than not.

Abe sat off to the side, reading *The Monthly Review*. He let the young woman stand at the counter while he finished reading an essay. It's a good idea to let customers stand and look for a few minutes, so they can decide what they are interested in. Although this young lady didn't look anything like a customer to Abe.

"Hey," she said at last.

Abe raised his eyebrows and looked at her over his glasses. Hey? Hey? This wasn't a grownup. Abe had been to lots of places, but he couldn't recall ever being addressed as "Hey" in all his years of teaching and all those demonstrations. "Yo" perhaps, but never "Hey." On the other hand, he had been in the store for ten years, and was probably out of touch. But still.

"May I help you?" Abe said. He stood and walked to the counter.

"I'm with *Allidos*. We are a confederation of community organizations, providing support for new immigrants and victims of hate crimes and state-sponsored violence in Rhode Island and southern New England," the young woman said. Her tongue was pierced too. She had a hint of an accent, but not one Abe could place.

"Uh huh," Abe said.

"We are doing a community picnic as a fundraiser to raise money for our anti-racist, anti-fascist work. Do you have any food or supplies you can donate? Either for the fundraiser or to help us care for undocumented families," the young woman said.

The young woman looked wild and crazy, but she talked like a college kid. There was something vaguely familiar about her. That was strange. Abe hadn't been around college kids in ten years, and for the ten years before that it had been mostly graduate students. His graduate students tended to be scruffy and intense. The women were partial to tight black tops and jeans, the men to leather jackets, and they all tried to look like they were working class. But not like this. No piercings.

"You go to RISD?" Abe said.

"Brown," the young woman said.

"This is a window treatment store. We sell mini-blinds. Curtains. Motorized window treatments. Stuff like that. Nothing of much use to undocumented people. Or that will be of any help in the anti-racist work, I'm afraid."

When Abe said the word "anti-racist", the young woman looked at him suspiciously, as though she had never heard an adult use that word before. Was he yanking her chain?

"Would you consider being a sponsor for the fundraiser? We have different levels—platinum, gold, silver, and bronze," the young woman said.

"Platinum, gold, and silver. Pretty capitalist language for anti-capitalist folks. Hierarchal structure, like the class system. Kind of a contradiction, don't you think?" Abe said.

The young woman looked at Abe like he had just walked out of a lunar lander. Human perhaps, but definitely from outer space. He was coming from a way different place than she expected. This was a wall-covering store.

"Huh. Brown. Where are you from? Bet you come from money yourself," Abe said. He had a sudden sense of déjà vu, as though this was a conversation he'd once had before, someplace in the distant past, or in a dream. The young woman had a certain mystery to her, a certain beauty that seemed oriental, as though a part of her was from a different culture and a part was intensely familiar. The pink and blue hair and the piercings were distractions from that beauty, but it was clearly there, despite the young woman's attempt to cover it up.

"And why do you think having picnics and fundraisers are going to get rid of racism?" Abe said. "Do you really believe you can go to a place like Brown, which was founded by slave traders, by god, and not be completely co-opted? Don't you know that's what Ivy League colleges are for? To take people with just a spark of intelligence, originality, and rebellion in them, and grind them down, burying them under volumes and volumes of academic claptrap and a zillion pages of distractionary rhetoric, to convince you that you are incapable of thinking for yourself."

"Say what?" the young woman said. "I came here to ask for a donation, not to get a lecture. You don't know the first thing about me. I might as well not be in the room. Who do you think you are?"

Huh, Abe thought. There's a little fight in this young woman after all, despite how she looks.

And at the same time, he thought, this feels familiar. I've had this argument before.

"What's your name, anyway? Where are you from?" Abe said.

"I'm Rose. Rose Levy. I'm from Cuernavaca. That's in Mexico," the young woman said. "And I come from culture, not from money. Full ride, if you must know. But my people are artists, potters and poets. And yes, I'm a Mexican Jew."

A door that had been closed suddenly opened.

Rose was Lily's granddaughter. Of all the little shops in America, of all the stores and restaurants and gas stations, Lily's granddaughter had walked into the stupid little store that Abe ran, almost fifty years after Lily left him. And then she had the same fight with Abe that Abe and Lily used to have. Fifty years before.

Abe was too much of a materialist to think that there must be a god to make something like that happen, but he thought it anyway, at least for a moment, until he pushed that thought away. There is a great synchrony in human affairs. Structural isomorphism. We are made a certain way. What brings us together once sometimes brings us together again. We are one people and joined at the hip, however much our greed and jealousies pull us apart. That is all logical and explainable. But there is also a coherence to our lives that feels unexplainable, that is deep and mysterious and very powerful all at the same time.

You could say Abe Klein took Rosie Levy under his wing, or you could say Rosie Levy brought Abe Klein back from the dead. Abe came to all Rosie's demonstrations. She wouldn't let him drive her places, but if they met at a demonstration, she would let him drive her home. And let him take her to Gregg's for coffee and dessert.

Abe sat down on the pavement with Rose at the demonstration

at the Wyatt when a truck tried to drive through the line and he got Maced with a hundred others. Rose stood next to him while he sat on the grass next to the road and held his head as the medics washed his eyes with water and milk, until he could see again, and she drove him home that night in his car.

They talked. Or she talked and he listened. He was tempted to teach her a little philosophy, a little Plato, a little Kant, a little Hegel, and a lot of Marx, but for once he kept his mouth shut.

She was young and full of dreams. There was nothing more Abe Klein wanted than to listen and feel her hope and energy, so he could dream again himself.

She told Abe all about her grandmother. Lily had never married. Her daughter Violetta was the child of a married gondolier Lily met in Venice, who had died 10 years before. Her life had been rich in family and in relationships, and she had never let herself be confined. Not to one man. One relationship. Or even one place or gender.

Soon Abe Facetimed with Lily, once, twice and then for a few minutes whenever he spent an hour or two with Rose. Lily hadn't changed. She had crow's feet around her eyes perhaps, but aside from that, she hadn't aged a day. Her eyes were still dark brown and almost black, and they seemed even more lustrous than ever, the door to a soul that was as deep as the sea and as glittering as the Milky Way.

Yes, she would come to Providence, she said, and Abe thought he could hear some excitement, and even a little yearning in her voice when she said that. But that was how she talked to everyone, to every man and woman she'd ever known. He'd be thrilled if she came, he said, and a part of him hoped she'd say, come here to visit. Come to Cuernavaca. But she didn't say that, and Abe was content to just see her and to hear her voice once again.

Abe was waiting for Lily's first visit when Covid hit. He is still waiting patiently until people can travel again. He listens, sees the world as it is, and is still the Blind Emperor, but is also now seeing and listening to the world as it is, not the way it was or the way he thinks it should be.

GLOSSARY

Aliyah—Literally, going up. Generally used to describe the honor of being asked to recite blessings before the reading of a portion of the Torah. There are generally eight such honors each time the Torah is read.

Amidah—Silent Prayer, the central prayer of Jewish liturgy, which usually consists of 18 blessings but the actual number said varies with time of day and day of the week. It is repeated at least three times a day during the week and four times on Saturday, and recited silently, standing up and facing east. When a minyan is present, it is usually repeated, chanted out loud by the person leading the service.

Baruchhamachers—Literally, the makers of blessings. Old observant men who would stand in Jewish cemeteries and read psalms for people who came visit the graves of loved ones, hoping for a little money in return for that service.

Baruch Hashem—Literally, blessed be the name. A phrase people say to indicate their recognition of and thankfulness for the blessings in their lives.

Bahur—first born son, a group who have an obligation to fast on the day before Passover, a fast that can be avoided by attending a special service in which a volume, or trachtate, or the Talmud is completed.

Beresheit—the Hebrew name of the book of Genesis.

Borachu—literally, blessing. A blessing repeated out loud early in each service, which functions as a call to prayer.

B'seder. Hebrew slang. It's okay. It's good. A contraction of Kol b'seder, everything is in order.

Daven—(verb) to pray.

El Malei Rach-amim—a Jewish prayer for the soul of a person who has died, asking that that soul be given proper rest. Usually recited at funerals, at gravesides and at memorial services.

Gabbai—the person who calls people to have the honor of saying blessings before the reading of the Torah.

Haysedonda—yiddishized contraction for "Hey, sit down there" a joking description of the shamesh.

Halacha—Jewish law

HIAS—Hebrew Immigrant Aid Society, an organization that looked after new Jewish immigrants a hundred years ago and again after the Second World War and the Holocaust, and then again when large numbers of Russian immigrants came to the US, in the 1980s and 1990s, and which advocates effectively for immigrants from many places today.

JCC—Jewish Community Center, usually a building which often has a gym and a swimming pool and meeting rooms for Jewish community organization, common in the larger Jewish communities of the US.

Kaddish—a prayer about the holiness of G-d, repeated a number of times in each service, and said standing by those in mourning and by people on the anniversary of the deaths of loved ones. The Mourner's Kaddish can only be said when a minyan (ten men, or ten people, depending on the congregation) is present.

Kaddish D'Rabbanan—a version of the Kaddish than recognizes the importance of scholars, recited in Orthodox communities after a lecture on certain parts of Talmud, and in other communities as part of the morning service.

Kiddusha—a section of the Amidah (Silent Prayer) which is recited only when a minyan is present.

Kippa (s), Kippas (pl)—skull cap, yarmulka.

Landsmannschraft—association of landsmen, of people from the same shtetl, or small town.

Lubavitcher—a member of the Hasidic community also known as Chabad, which began in Lubavitch, in White Russia, in 1775, came to the US after the Second World War, and is headquartered on Eastern Parkway in Brooklyn. It was led in the United States by Rabbi Menachem Mendel Schneerson (1902-1994). There are just as many conflicts and controversies in the Hasidic movement and among observant Jews as there are in other faith communities. Not all observant people hold the Lubavitcher movement in high regard.

Maariv—the evening service, often combined with Mincha, the afternoon service.

Mincha—the afternoon service.

Minyan—traditionally, the ten men required for a service that includes saying a number of important prayers out loud or at all and for reading the Torah. US conservative and reform congregations now count all people over thirteen or who have been bar or bat mitzvahed as constituting a minyan.

Misheberach—(literally, blessing) used here to mean the blessing for the one's family.

Parasha Vayera—the portion named Vayera. The Torah, the Five Books of Moses, is comprised of five books. Each book is divided into weekly portions, or parshiyot (plural, parasha - singular). There are 54 parshiyot in all, each about long enough to consume about an hour of time when they are read aloud quickly. Jews all over the world read the same parasha each week. Many Jews in Europe used the weekly parasha instead of a calendar because everyone knew the time of year each parasha was (and is) read. Each parasha is named, usually for its first word or phrase. Vayera is Hebrew for *and He appeared*. It is the fourth parasha of the year, the fourth parasha in the book of Beresheit, or Genesis, and the fourth parasha to be read after the holiday of Simchat Torah, which is celebrated 23 days after Rosh Hashanah, so usually in the Julian calendar month of October or November.

Pikuach nefesh—A principle of Jewish law derived from Torah and developed in the Talmud, that says other Jewish laws can be violated if doing so is necessary to save a life.

Shtiebela—tiny store-front synagogue, common in the Lower East Side of New York from 1900 until about 1950, and in the Jewish cities of Eastern Europe.

Shema—A one line prayer that serves as the central coda of Judaism. "Hear O Israel the Lord our G-d, the Lord is One" is a rough translation. It is repeated at least twice a day, is said by children as a bedtime prayer, and observant Jews try to have it on their lips at the moment of their deaths.

Shmoneh esrei—the Amidah, or Silent Prayer.

Shul—Yiddish colloquialism for synagogue.

Sephardic trope—the sung pronunciation of the Torah read in Hebrew used by Jews descended from those who lived in Spain and Portugal, communities that moved to Holland, Greece, Turkey, Italy and North Africa after the Spanish Inquisition. That pronunciation used by Jews in Eastern Europe is called Ashkenazi trope.

Shabbat Shalom—tradition shabbos greeting, literally, greetings/peace on this Sabbath.

Shabbos—The Sabbath, the central organizing feature of Jewish life.

Shamesh—traditionally, the warden or caretaker of the synagogue.

Now used to describe the person who organizes a religious service. Originally and also the candle on a Hanukah menorah that is used to light all the other candles, which is the origin of the use of the word in synagogue life.

Shaharit—the morning service

Shtetl—Small Yiddish speaking community in Eastern Europe. The villages where Jews lived, next to but other separate from their non-Jewish neighbors.

Siddur—prayer book, singular Siddurim (plural)

Talmud—63 complicated books of what was originally oral law that was transcribed to text, commentaries on that law and stories about the law and the (thousands of) rabbis who complied it over many centuries, all developed from the law set out in the Torah.

Tallesim (plural) Talis, singular, Askenazi; Tallit, singular, Sephardic—prayer shawl, worn on shabbos.

Torah—The five books of Moses, written by a trained scribe's hand on a sheepskin scroll, which is read out loud on Monday, Thursday and Saturday (Shabbos). There is considerable ceremony attached to the reading of the Torah, and a significant body of Jewish law laying out the way it is to be read. Once upon a time, the law was read in the marketplace: Monday and Thursday were market days.

Yahrzeit—the anniversary of the death of a close (parent child or spouse) loved one, when Kaddish is recited in the presence of a minyan.

Yiddishe Kupp—Literally, a Yiddish, or Jewish head. An expression that means a person has the ability to think clearly, with the benefit of Jewish wisdom, and from the perspective of Jewish history and experience.

Yiskor—a prayer service in which the dead are remembered, recited four times a year.

ACKNOWLEDGEMENTS

The author gratefully acknowledges the help of Penney Stein, ace proofreader, Brianna Benjamin, for editorial support, Gabriel Fine, for comments and thoughts on Jewish ideas and concepts and for help making sure that how I used contemporary Hebrew is in fact contemporary, and to many readers, teachers and colleagues, for feedback and inspiration, and to Carol Levitt-Fine and Rosie Fine, for support and encouragement. All mistakes are my own.

ABOUT THE AUTHOR

Michael Fine is a writer, community organizer, family physician, public health official, and author of *Health Care Revolt: How to Organize, Build a Health Care System, and Resuscitate Democracy—All at the Same Time*, *On Medicine As Colonialism*, and *Abundance*, a romantic thriller set in Rhode Island and in Liberia in the aftermath of the Liberian Civil Wars of 1989-2003. He has authored two other short story collections, *The Bull* and *Rhode Island Stories*.

All of Michael Fine's stories and books are available at www.MichaelFineMD.com.

ALSO BY MICHAEL FINE

ABUNDANCE

Julia is an American medical doctor fleeing her own privileged background to find a new live delivering healthcare to African villages, where her skills can make a difference. Carl is also an American, whose very experiences as a black man in the United States have driven him into exile in West Africa, where he is an international NGO expat. The two come together as colleagues (and then more) as Liberia is gripped in a brutal civil war. Child soldiers kidnap Julia on a remote jungle road, and Carl is evacuated against his will by U.S. Marines. Back in the United States he finds Julia's mentor, Levin, a

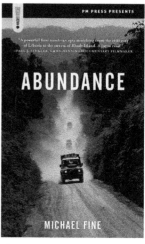

Rhode Island MD whose Sixties idealism has been hijacked by history They meet the thief. Then they meet the smuggler. And the dangerous work of finding and rescuign Julia begins.

THE BULL AND OTHER STORIES

A bull gets loose in Tennessee. black sergeant stops the murder of a Trump supporter in North Carolina. The third husband of a nurse in Pawtucket wins the lottery. A schizophrenic woman who lives on Kennedy Plaza discovers that Social Security thinks she is dead. The 19-year-old Latina caretaker of a rich old man loses her mother to COVID-19. A horse that represents the hopes and dreams of a family in India falls asleep, and then awakens.

Ten stories. People whose lives are transformed. People who struggle and survive, who see their world through lost hopes, inappropriate loves, and irrational dreams. Ten stories, each one a new way to listen, see, feel and dream.

Rhode Island Stories

Rhode Island. A tiny little state with more
stories than people. Hopes and dreams, sick-
nesses, deaths and disappointments. Loves and
heartbreaks. Some of us trying to repair the
world. Others overwhelmed by the beauty of
the world as it is. All in one place, becoming
one people. What democracy looks like.

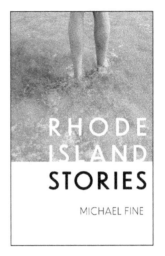

Printed in the USA
CPSIA information can be obtained
at www.ICGtesting.com
JSHW040007150224
57156JS00015B/48/J